'No you're not, Ethel. I'm ⎡...⎤ thought, when I talked to ⎡...⎤ kind of girl who could enjo⎡...⎤ a mistake . . .'

She recalled Bennie's note: *I realize now that I made a terrible mistake*. Bennie had. William hadn't.

'It's . . .' She stared at her drink, swirled it, looked at him. 'I should be having the time of my life, William. Truth is, I've got a big problem an' it's playin' on me mind.'

'Then tell me about it.'

She explained. She left out nothing . . .

By the same author

*The Outsider*
*The Dark Side of the Sun*

EastEnders Novels

*Home Fires Burning*
*Swings and Roundabouts*
*Good Intentions*

# HUGH MILLER

# The Flower of
# Albert Square

## EastEnders – Book 4

*By arrangement with the
British Broadcasting Corporation*

**GRAFTON BOOKS**

A Division of the Collins Publishing Group

LONDON GLASGOW
TORONTO SYDNEY AUCKLAND

Grafton Books
A Division of the Collins Publishing Group
8 Grafton Street, London W1X 3LA

A Grafton Paperback Original 1986

ISBN 0-586-06812-0

Printed and bound in Great Britain by
Collins, Glasgow

Set in Times

# PART ONE
# Before

# 1

All the way from the tube station the smoke and swirling dust had been growing thicker, drifting in waves on the sultry afternoon air. At a corner by a boarded-up pork butcher's shop Ethel stopped, trying to guess where the latest doodlebug had landed. There was a hovering dark patch high in the sky over by Royal College Street; it could be St Pancras Station that had caught it, or one of the warehouses near there. Ethel began walking again, flapping a hand in front of her face to deflect the tendrils of sooty smoke.

Halfway along Crowndale Road she noticed that the darkness in the sky had shifted as she changed direction; it looked much closer than before. Fifty yards from the turning into Beryl Avenue she saw that the light was wrong, somehow. At that time of day the rows of houses should be casting long shadows into the road. But they weren't. There was a wedge of yellowy sunlight across the pitted tarmac. As she got nearer she heard noise; clanking metal, the grind of stones being shifted, men shouting. Ethel began to walk faster.

She turned the corner and stumbled to a halt. It was all wrong. This wasn't where she lived. Instead of houses there were shapeless islands of smoking rubble. Firemen stood in the brick-strewn roadway, playing their hoses on hissing tangles of steel, wood and masonry. People in uniforms were scurrying around like ants, clambering over bulwarks of smashed tiles and twisted railings. High above them, the pall of dark smoke hung like a sombre marker.

Ethel jerked her stunned gaze across the devastation,

7

trying to find a bearing. For most of her twenty-four years she had known the geography of Beryl Avenue intimately. She knew all the people who lived there. But now she saw none of those people. Their houses were gone and strangers with gaunt faces were burrowing in the remains. It took a minute for Ethel's bewilderment to give way to a fluttering of panic.

'Mum?'

She stumbled forward, trying to pinpoint number 38. She saw something familiar, one green gate-post standing up at the centre of a pile of earth and shredded turf. She rushed across and touched it. The house had stood no more than ten feet behind the post. Now there was a cavernous mound of jagged debris, with half the front door visible in a dull-glinting pool of smashed glass.

'Oh, God . . .'

A tin-hatted man appeared beside her, reaching out as she swayed. 'Steady, love.' He put an arm around her shoulder and led her to the middle of the road. 'There's still some pockets of gas. Better stay well back.' He was nearly a foot taller than Ethel. As he turned her to face him she saw from his buttons and collar numbers that he was a policeman. His smile was sad. 'You from round here, are you?'

She glanced back at the place where the house had been that morning when she left. 'There,' she croaked, pointing.

Now it was all spinning in her head, the recollection of an ordinary Saturday morning. Her mother doing the ironing, Dad in the corner with the big iron last on his knees, putting a rubber heel on a boot. They had hardly looked up as she went out. 'Don't be late back,' her mother had said. Ethel was nearly an hour early. For once, she was back in time for tea.

'What number, love?' The policeman was taking a notebook from his pocket.

'Thirty-eight.' Ethel swallowed hard. 'Has – has the ambulance been?' None of this seemed real. Not yet. They had survived the nightmare of the Blitz. They'd been talking about the end of the war, only the night before. 1944 was the big turning point: it would all be over soon.

'Name of Trent – is that it?'

Ethel nodded.

Before he spoke again the constable seemed to rehearse something with silent-moving lips. 'Two people at home, a man and a woman. Would that be right?'

'My mum and dad.'

A young woman in a blue dress and black-belted white apron came across from the rubble on the other side of the avenue. She wore a tin helmet like the constable's. He looked relieved to see her.

'What's happened to them?' Ethel asked.

The policeman cleared his throat. 'This nurse'll take you to the Warden's Post, love. They've got some nice hot tea . . .'

'What about Mum and Dad?'

'There, ah . . . There were no survivors at all, I'm afraid. It was a direct hit.'

No survivors. Ethel turned that around in her mind. 'But . . .'

'Sorry, love.'

The nurse took Ethel's arm and began leading her away. Following, Ethel tried to cope with the information in a way that wouldn't mean anything bad. No survivors. It could mean nobody got off scot free. But the policeman hadn't said that. And he had something about her parents in his book.

She stopped suddenly, staring at the nurse as an icy fear gripped her. 'Are they dead?'

The girl had a tired, kindly face. 'Come on, dear. I'll get you a hot drink.'

9

They moved past the ambulances, vans and trucks of the rescue services, parked in an impotent huddle beside the only two remaining buildings at the end of the avenue. There was a mobile canteen set up beside the Warden's Post. Ethel let the nurse ease her down on to an upended crate. She saw a few familiar faces around her. They all looked shocked and distant. One young man was crying softly as he tried to drink from a mug.

It was too unreal. The dread she had felt a minute ago had inched away, leaving her puzzled. It was hard to make any sense of what had happened. She had no parents; that wasn't a thing she could make herself believe. The house was gone. The avenue was gone. Ethel felt herself shiver, even though the day was warm.

The tea was brought by a woman in a dark blue uniform with three stripes on the jacket cuff. She made sure Ethel was holding the cup with both hands before she let go.

'Do you feel up to giving me some particulars?' she asked.

Ethel looked at her. When people asked for particulars she always thought of the bits of paper she carried in her handbag. Her particulars. It dawned sharply that beyond her particulars and a few other things in the bag, she had nothing at all now.

'What's your full name?' The woman had a clipboard poised, her pencil hovering.

'Ethel May Trent.'

'And your address?'

Ethel told her, along with her age and her occupation – part-time war work.

'Do you have any other relatives?'

'Yes.'

Now this was something she wanted to go back on. Right back to half an hour ago when she got on the tube. If she'd stayed where she was, wandered about for a while, maybe walked home, this wouldn't have happened. This would be cancelled. The avenue, the house, her parents, they would still be there.

Somewhere off to the north of the city there was a rumbling explosion. The woman with the clipboard watched the sky for a moment, then looked back at Ethel.

'What other relatives, love?'

She had a sister who'd been evacuated. They hadn't heard from her in a while. One brother in the army somewhere, another who had never come back from Dunkirk. The information didn't seem to be of much use to the woman.

'I've an auntie and uncle and cousins in Hackney.'

'Address?'

They lived somewhere near Colesgrave Road, Ethel remembered. She wasn't sure of the address. It had been a couple of years since she had seen any of them. They weren't all that close, as families went.

'Try and think,' the woman said. It wasn't impatience that put the urgency in her voice. She was trying to get the information before shock got a firm hold on Ethel. In this case, her experience told her, the full weight of grief would be delayed. Being bereaved and bombed-out on the same day was something that took different people in different ways.

Ethel opened her handbag and pulled out the penny calendar with the address pages at the back. She handed it to the woman. 'I think they're in there . . .'

Something happened just after that. Ethel saw the cup slipping from her fingers. She couldn't do anything to stop it, she didn't even feel she wanted to. Everything around her seemed to tilt. She felt hands on her shoulders and at her waist, then she knew she was being lifted. She believed she saw the rest, but everything was disjointed, without meaning or any sense of time.

11

What she was conscious of, next, was a Ministry of Food poster. She was lying on a spindly, metal-framed bed in a makeshift shelter in some basement or other. There were a lot of other beds in there, mostly with people lying on them. The poster was on the wall beside Ethel. It had a picture of a fat man and a woman on it and alongside there was a rhyme:

> *Reflect when ever you indulge*
> *It is not beautiful to bulge*
> *A large untidy corporation*
> *Is far from helpful to the nation.*

That one had always made her dad laugh, she remembered. He had even memorized the words.

'How are you feeling now?' A man with a white coat and a Red-Cross armband was standing by the bed.

'All right, thank you.' Ethel wasn't sure how she felt. Her tongue clicked on her palate, and her eyes felt as if they were crusted with dried tears.

'There's somebody here to see you.'

The man stepped aside and an older man came forward. He had a look of mingled pity, regret and embarrassment. Uncle George had never been very fond of her, Ethel knew that. He'd told her mother she was too flighty for her own good.

'A terrible business, Ethel.' He shook his head and twisted the brim of his hat, which he was holding in front of him. 'Your Aunt and me . . .' He waved his hand vaguely to finish the sentence. 'Anyway, you can come back to our place.'

Ethel blinked up at him. 'I've got no things,' she said. 'Everything was in the house.' All gone, she thought. Every treasured trinket, every stitch of clothing. She couldn't imagine it being true, but it must be.

'We'll sort something out,' Uncle George said gruffly.

12

No mother, no father. It seemed that a long, happy, carefree time had come to an end. Nobody and nothing left. It was terribly odd. The world she knew had been obliterated and now, whether she wanted to or not, she would have to start all over again. Ethel looked down. Through eyes growing misty, she saw that her hands were shaking.

# 2

Herbert Lamb had been invalided out of the Royal Air Force in 1943 when a bomb-loader had trapped his right foot and crushed a couple of bones. He had come home with a limp, a brooding nature and a leaning towards the darker aspects of Christianity. Today, like most afternoons, he sat in the parlour with books piled on the table by his chair, occasionally pausing in his reading to gaze out at the street of drab, uniform houses.

'People get no better,' he mumbled as his mother dusted around him. It was a sunny afternoon in August, but Herbert's expression was more suited to drizzle.

'What's that then, Herbert?' Lily rarely met his gaze, which she always found accusing.

'That woman across the road. Mrs Lawton.'

'Oh, she's just a poor soul. She's had worry heaped on worry this past year – and more than her share of hardship.' Lily always tried to be charitable. 'Two sons missin', her girl off in the Land Army when she'd be better employed lookin' after her sick Dad, no real money comin' into the house . . .'

'You'd think she'd see the error of her ways.'

Lily looked at her son. In the fleeting second that her glance met his, she registered his sour mouth, the row of pimples on his pasty forehead, his narrow, red-rimmed eyes. He had been such a cheerful child. She often wondered at the change. Young men worse-off had fared a lot better.

'She's not a bad woman,' Lily said, resuming her dusting.

'Depends what you call bad.' He was twenty-three, but

14

he spoke like a patriarch. 'She's always gadding about the place and smiling at strange men.' Herbert adjusted the book on his knee and sighed.

'She makes an effort to keep herself cheery. Better than broodin' all day long.'

'I can see what she's up to,' he snorted. 'She's turning her back on her responsibilities and the simple rules of plain decency.'

'How do you make that out?'

'Her husband's lying in there on his sickbed, isn't he? Where is she most of the time? Out and about, looking for a good time.'

Lily rolled her eyes at the ceiling and put a little more elbow-drive behind her duster. Herbert was an odd one, even a mother had to admit that. He didn't even speak like the rest of the family. He had come back from the forces with a strained, high-pitched, artificial-sounding accent, a voice that reminded Lily of old ladies trying to talk posh whenever they addressed a vicar or school-teacher. As for the eternal bee in his bonnet about people's morals – well, Lily found that downright unhealthy.

'And here comes Jezebel herself.'

Lily turned and looked out of the window. Young Ethel was coming along the street. She was heavily made-up, as usual, her lipstick and rouge so vivid they looked like stuck-on patches of colour. Her hair was in elaborate Veronica Lake bangs and in spite of the warm weather she had on her astrakhan jacket. The tight tubular skirt seemed to make her hobble and her high-heeled, sling-back shoes looked very precarious.

'Don't go on at her,' Lily warned Herbert. 'She's been a bit better this week.'

'Better than what?'

'Herbert. She's still under the doctor. Just try givin'

her some of that Christian charity you're forever goin' on about.'

Herbert curled a lip towards his cousin as she came in through the gate. By the time she entered the parlour his eyes were fixed on his book again.

'Well then,' Aunt Lily said, her big, plain, friendly face brightening with visible effort. 'Had a nice walk round, have you?'

Ethel nodded. 'Went a bit further this time. It wasn't bad at all.'

Since the bomb fell at Beryl Avenue two months before, Ethel had suffered an overlapping series of nervous complaints. One of them, a form of agoraphobia, had made her afraid to go further than the front gate. With the help of her cousin Wendy and a complicated course of tablets and capsules, she had managed to overcome her fear. Or almost.

'I was a bit shaky when Wendy left me at the factory. But I got better after a bit.'

'That's the way.' Lily saw the edgy way Ethel was looking at Herbert. 'Let's go through an' make a cup of tea, then. I'm parched an' I'm sure you are, too.'

'If I can just pop upstairs for a minute . . .'

'Of course you can, love. This is your home now, I keep tellin' you that. Do what you feel like doin'.'

In her room, Ethel closed the door and leaned on it for a moment, listening to the sound of her blood pulsing in her ears. She was glad to be back, safe within these four walls, shut away from all the threats outside. But it really was better now, she hadn't lied to her aunt.

'Every day, a little bit better,' she murmured. The doctor had told her to keep telling herself that. 'Better an' better all the time.'

Now, after the panic and tears and nameless terrors she'd known at the beginning, she could walk along the streets and tell herself it was all right, nothing bad would happen. On each trip out she knew she was that little bit stronger, that tiny shade more confident. At odd moments, though, she would take sudden stock of herself; it wasn't deliberate, it simply happened and it frightened her. She would stop walking and pretend to look in shop windows or over bridges or just up at the sky, trembling with the sense of isolation, the terrible lonely feeling of being abandoned. Today it had happened only once. Afterwards, walking back to the house, she had begun to admit a new fear. Less a fear, perhaps, than a growing misery. She didn't think it had anything to do with her nerves.

'Tea'll be ready in five minutes,' Aunt Lily called from downstairs. 'I've got some biscuits for a treat.'

'Righto,' Ethel called.

She took off her jacket and hung it up. At the mirror she patted her hair and checked the gloss on her lipstick. It was funny how much more confident she felt with the make-up on. Before, she hadn't worn it much. She hadn't dressed up very often, either. The first thing she did, though, when they told her how much money there was from her mother and father, was to go out and buy clothes and lots of make-up, mostly from the black market people who accosted passers-by from the alleyways between buildings.

She opened the dressing-table drawer and fumbled beneath a pile of underwear. She found the half bottle of rum and unscrewed the cap quickly. This was something else she hadn't done before. Drink was something she could take or leave. Nowadays, a nip or two in the afternoon and a couple at night helped to keep her calm.

As she opened the door to go downstairs, the new fear or misery or whatever it was came at her again. He would be there, silently disapproving, making her feel like an interloper. Today, coming back along the street, she had felt that the whole squat mass of the house was him,

17

Herbert, frowning and resentful. For a few moments as she approached the gate, staying out had seemed a better idea than going indoors.

Aunt Lily had taken a trolley into the parlour. Her husband, George, always insisted that afternoon tea and late-evening supper should be served from a trolley. It was one of the genteel refinements befitting the household of a man in his position. He was, after all, a senior clerk in an ordnance factory, a position to which he had been catapulted by the heavy conscription of younger men. George liked his domestic arrangements to reflect his professional standing.

'Help yourself to a ginger snap,' Aunt Lily told Ethel. 'Herbert? Do you want a biscuit with your tea?'

Herbert pretended to surface from the engrossing text on his lap. 'Sorry? What did you say?'

'A biscuit. Do you want one?'

His lips slid slowly across each other, suggesting delicate distaste. 'Did we get them on the ration?'

Lily stared at him. 'What do you think?'

He sniffed. 'I think I want no part of ill-gotten goods. A cup of tea will do nicely.'

Lily began pouring. 'Take two, if you want,' she told Ethel, who had just put a biscuit on her plate.

The ten-minute ordeal that followed made Ethel glad that she'd taken a stiffener from the bottle before she came down. Herbert – he had flown off the handle at Ethel once for calling him Herbie – had made a variety of veiled references to the evils of the black market, the general public's feeble moral fibre and the iniquity of people who sponged off others. This last, Ethel knew, was a dig at herself. Herbert had never wanted her in the house, and as the days passed it became clear that he would never accept her as one of the family.

'Just get on with your tea,' his mother had told him

finally. 'If we want sermons, me an' Ethel can get our coats on an' pop down the church.'

Herbert looked incensed. 'That remark was in very poor taste,' he told his mother.

'Like most of the remarks that's been flyin' about here this afternoon.' Lily's rugged intelligence and ready tongue were a constant pain to Herbert. She was forever taking the edge off his biting observations.

'I'm entitled to my views,' he muttered.

Lily looked at him. For the first time, Ethel saw the dislike. 'If you exercised as much muscle as you do mouth, our Herbert, you'd be walkin' as straight as any man.'

He threw his book to the floor, making Ethel jump. 'So. It's not enough that I get maimed in the service of my country – I have to sit here and be mocked by my own mother, and in front of a stranger at that.'

'There's no strangers here,' Lily said sharply. 'Just you bear that in mind, young man.'

Herbert slapped down his cup and saucer on the chairside table. 'I choose to think differently.'

'You choose when you're in a position to choose!'

'And what does that mean?'

'It means,' Lily said, her cheeks turning crimson, 'that when you're payin' your way, like everybody else in this house, you'll have earned the right to open your trap the way you do.'

Herbert shot to his feet and hobbled to the centre of the room. 'That was unforgiveable!'

Ethel looked at him sidelong. He was mad, she was sure of it. He talked weird, he postured like he was a lord's son and he had the too-moist, furtive eyes she saw on men in the waiting room at the clinic she attended every week. Something about Herbert – everything about him, really – made her realize she wasn't as far gone in her head as a lot of people. She glanced away quickly as his tremulous gaze fell on her.

'And what are *you* gawping at?'

'I wasn't gawpin',' Ethel said huskily.

'Leave her,' Lily warned. It was the first time there had been an open confrontation in Ethel's presence, although she had sometimes heard raised voices when she was up in her room. 'If you've finished with that tea,' Lily went on, 'I suggest you go out an' get some air about you.'

'I don't feel well enough to go out!' There was a whine in Herbert's voice that was reminiscent of a petulant, self-pitying child. 'Walks are for people with imaginary ailments, anyway!'

'That is *enough*!' Lily snapped. 'Ethel, bring your tea. We'll have ours in the kitchen.' She stood up and braced both hands on the trolley. 'We'll leave this one to cough on his own fumes.'

In the kitchen they stood by the draining board, staring out at the back garden. George, a dedicated digger for victory, had regimented the small stretch into rectangular vegetable plots with narrow grassy margins. The tidiness always soothed Ethel, who had never managed to organize anything in her life.

'You're not to let Herbert get you down,' Lily said at last. 'He's got his own problems an' he likes takin' them out on other folk. Not that he means the half of what he says, I suppose.'

Ethel nodded, pretending to understand. Since she had been there, she had been acutely aware of two waves of feeling towards her. Aunt Lily and Wendy both liked her. They were sympathetic about her loss and the nervous trouble she had suffered since. Uncle George and Herbert, on the other hand, didn't really care for her. They certainly didn't like her staying at their house.

'I try not to get in Herbert's way,' she told her aunt.

'An' when I can get workin' again an' sort meself out proper, I'll get a place of me own. I think it'd be best.'

Lily looked at her gravely. 'Listen to me, my girl. You're my sister's child. I loved my sister an' there's not a day passes but I don't miss her.' She hesitated before going on. 'These past ten years we weren't close. No fault of mine or your mum's. Your Uncle George has these fixed ideas, see. Him an' your dad didn't hit it off, an' because of that, an' other things, we drifted. But my sister an' her kids was never out of my mind. Never.'

'Mum thought about you a lot, too.'

Lily stared bitterly at the garden. 'Menfolk. They're not worth a tenth the trouble we go to because of them. We give in right an' left, put up with their flamin' moods . . .' She gulped her tea and looked at Ethel again. 'You're as much kin to me as my own family, Ethel. Don't forget it. As long as you're here you're welcome. If anybody tries to make you feel any way else, they'll have me to settle with.'

After dinner that evening, Ethel spent an hour in her room, sorting out the clothes from her drawers and the cupboard, rehanging and folding them as she did most nights. Her thoughts drifted easily at those times; she was sure it had something to do with the two capsules she had to swallow at six o'clock. The thoughts that came and went never hurt, although some of them were sad. She kept picturing childhood days with her sister and brothers. A lot of the time she thought about her parents, a good, hard-working, cheerful couple, full of Cockney humour and toughness.

'Got to have a direction in life, girl,' she whispered, imagining her father's voice and seeing his face as she said it. 'No use chuggin' around every which way. Get yourself on the right rails, then don't shift off that line.'

They had been her rails, her father and mother. They had been the guides towards wherever she was going.

And now? Without rails, she felt no sense of direction. She was adrift. Or bogged down. Ethel couldn't decide.

She liked to remember the songs her dad sang. He was always good at memorizing words and mimicking voices. She sat by her bed with a couple of dresses spread across the counterpane, patting out small creases as she hummed her way through *South American Joe*, then *These Foolish Things*, then *Over My Shoulder*.

She hung up the dresses in the cupboard and stood looking across the room. Tonight she felt restless. It was Herbert's fault, she believed. Even though she couldn't see or hear him, she knew he'd be sitting downstairs, or in his room, disliking her and wishing she wasn't there. His outburst that afternoon had unsettled her. She couldn't dislike him too much because she was so sure he was mad and couldn't help himself, but she couldn't feel too comfortable, either, knowing he was there.

Wendy was working late at the factory. There was always Aunt Lily to talk to, but that would mean being where Uncle George was, with his rattling newspaper and his own brand of unspoken disapproval.

Ethel looked at the drawer with the bottle in it. She had half decided to have a drink when she stopped. What she really fancied was going out somewhere. The thought of being outside at night didn't trouble her. The dark was like something safe she could wrap around her.

The decision was one of the firmest she had made in a long time. She set out clothes on the bed – her brightest, the yellow frock and the mustard cardigan with the embroidered flower on it – and began to get ready. The make-up would take a long time, she thought, but she would enjoy putting it on. She always did.

In half an hour she was ready. She stood before the long mirror on the inside of the cupboard door, turning her shoulders one way then the other, smiling at her reflection. The little brown hat with the wisp of gold net had been an afterthought. She thought it looked very good with the rest of her outfit – and the white shoes were definitely the right touch.

At the foot of the stairs she met Uncle George, heading for the parlour with his newspaper. When she was small, she remembered, he had always gone about the house in his shirtsleeves with his braces dangling. Nowadays he wore a waistcoat, all done up except for the bottom button.

'Off out, are you?' he grunted. The frown told her just what he thought about the way she looked.

'To see some friends,' Ethel said, nodding. It wasn't entirely untrue; she had already met a few of the people who used the pub two streets away, which was where she had decided she would go.

He nodded curtly and moved on along the hallway ahead of her. 'Won't be late, will you? Your aunt and me turn in early. Don't like getting disturbed . . .'

'I won't be late.'

As she was going out through the front door she heard him clearly, his voice carrying as he closed the parlour door. 'You should just see the sight of that,' he said. 'God knows what people must think.'

Ethel didn't feel offended. What he didn't understand was that people actually liked her to dress up brightly, and to put on heavy make-up. She knew they liked it because it made them talk to her. She was never stuck for a conversation when she went out looking like this.

Something else occurred to her as she teetered along the street in her spiky high heels. The thought wasn't too clear, but she knew it had a seed of the truth in it. She believed she dressed up gaudily and put herself behind a mask of cosmetics because it gave her some notion of herself; she felt she was *somebody*. Bare-faced and wrapped in her dressing gown, she could look at herself and see no one at all.

23

# 3

At the beginning of October the British people learned that Mr Churchill was making a ten-day visit to Moscow. At approximately the same time Russian and Yugoslav troops entered Belgrade and the American Army landed in the Philippines. The war was on its last legs, everyone said so. A lot of famous people wouldn't see the end, however; that year Stephen Leacock died, and so did Sir Henry Wood, Sir Arthur Quiller-Couch and Heath Robinson. Rommel died too, reinforcing the feeling in Britain that the whole German war machine was falling apart.

International events made little impact on Ethel. She knew things were getting better because people said so. She was influenced more by propaganda than the network of facts that spelled imminent victory. She had begun going to the cinema and saw inspiring films like *Stage Door Canteen*, *Mrs Miniver* and *Coastal Command*. She also saw *Henry V*, but she didn't understand it and fell asleep before the end. The message on every hand, it seemed, was that the long night of war was shifting towards dawn.

Ethel began to daydream about what it would be like to live in a world of peace. For her, she suspected, things might not be much different. Life had settled to a routine again; it wasn't as happy a routine as she'd had before the V1 rocket wiped out Beryl Avenue, but it was a pattern of living that felt like it might last.

It was also a pattern that caused tension between Uncle George and Aunt Lily. On a bitterly cold evening in early November, as George sat by one side of the fireplace reading his newspaper, while Lily sat opposite with her darning and Herbert pored over a book at the table, the front door clicked shut. It was half-past seven. The door closed behind Ethel at that time almost every evening now. George lowered his paper and glanced accusingly at his wife. Herbert tutted softly. Lily went on darning.

'It's really getting to be too much,' George said. Like his son, he had recently adopted a clipped, tight-throated manner of speech, an attempt to simulate the voice of urban respectability. 'What decent girl goes out at this hour every night?'

Lily looked at him. 'Ethel does, for one.'

Herbert snorted quietly.

'Decent, I said. Do you call that kind of behaviour decent?' George had a long, thin face that could switch from displeasure to affront in an instant. 'Do you?'

Lily glanced briefly towards Herbert, making it clear that she was reluctant to say what was on her mind while their son was present.

'You really surprise me, Lily,' George went on. 'You defend that girl and condone her actions at every turn. You act as if you can't see what's going on.'

'I can't. You tell me what's goin' on.'

'Oh, for heaven's sake – '

'You seem to know so much about it.'

Herbert was watching them, a thin smile twisting his mouth.

'You know perfectly well what I mean. And the gossip will centre on this house, let me remind you. *Our home.*'

'Gossip about what?' Lily demanded.

'Her!'

'She's doin' no harm. Can you prove she is? Has she done one thing to hurt you or me or anybody since she came here? Eh?'

George rattled his newspaper down on his knees. 'She's

25

harming our reputation, Lily. We're decent people who don't hold with that kind of thing.'

Lily shook her head. 'Decent. It's your favourite word lately. An' what's this about "we" all the time? What is it "we" aren't supposed to hold with?'

'Sluttish behaviour, that's what. She goes about looking like a harlot all the time, and every night she's out roaming the streets like some . . .' He cut off sharply, glancing at Herbert. 'I happen to know she uses the pubs round here.'

'We've been known to use them ourselves, from time to time.'

'That isn't the point. She dolls herself up deliberately to attract men's attention, then she goes flaunting herself in public bars . . .'

Herbert cleared his throat. '"Thine eyes shall behold strange women",' he said, '"and thine heart shall utter perverse things."'

George and Lily looked at him.

Herbert smiled tightly. '"They that tarry long at the wine – "'

'Shut up, you,' Lily snapped.

'Don't go picking on him,' George hissed, 'when you won't say a word against that little strumpet.'

Lily shoved her darning into the cloth bag beside her and placed her hands firmly on the arms of her chair. 'Right. I'll say something about her. And about you lot while I'm at it.' She looked slowly from one to the other, letting her eyes rest on George. 'Ethel's been through a terrible time,' she said, 'a nightmare of a time, what with losin' her parents an' her home an' everythin' she owned. On top of it all she's suffered with her nerves. In spite of all that, she's worked hard at gettin' herself straight. She goes about this place like a mouse, botherin' nobody, helpin' where she can, doin' everythin' in her power to please.'

'I'm not saying that's not true – '

'I'm not finished, George. She's got herself a job now an' she pays her way – not that she didn't before. Since Wendy's been away workin' in Portsmouth it's been double lonely for Ethel, so she's been goin' out a lot more – dressed the way she wants an' the way she's got a right to dress, if it pleases her . . .'

'Like some painted gipsy . . .'

Lily leaned forward, glaring at her husband. 'You want to bear in mind that she's not some little kid – she's a grown woman of near twenty-five. She has every right to do what she wants, as long as she's hurtin' nobody.'

Herbert tutted again.

'As for you,' Lily said, turning on him, 'you do nothin' but sit around on your behind, face stuck in a book all the time, only speakin' when you feel like snipin' at somebody. You do nothin',' ever. An' before you start tellin' me how much you sacrificed for your country, let me remind you there's them that sacrificed a damn sight more. Ethel did. An' not deliberately neither.'

Herbert's eyes began to jerk between his mother and father. His face reddened.

'I'm not goin' into all that,' Lily assured him. 'I'm just remindin' you not to chuck stones unless you know you've a right.'

The matter of Herbert's visitors from the Air Force a year ago, the stern voices behind the closed parlour door, the accusing tone of the officer with all the silver braid, then the string of grim brown envelopes marked STRICTLY PRIVATE – that had been endured without comment.

'I don't know what Ethel gets up to when she's not here – none of us knows. It's charitable, I reckon, to think the best when you don't know the facts.' Looking pointedly at Herbert, she added, 'It's what I do.'

Where her son was concerned, all Lily knew was that

he had been no innocent victim of a straightforward accident. She had heard the phrase 'working his ticket' more than once during this war, and she knew what it meant. George must have had heavy suspicions, too, but he probably submerged them beneath the outward evidence – his lad was a semi-cripple, a victim of the war. Despite her own self-delusion, Lily occasionally dwelt on Herbert's official discharge from the forces; no commendations, no expressions of sympathy or regret. He was simply out, without a pension.

George looked as if he was getting ready to say something. Lily headed him off. 'As for the harm Ethel's doin' to our respectable reputation,' she said, 'that's all in your head, George. We're plain folk livin' on a plain old street. A half dozen girls just like Ethel live round here. Nobody goes on about them.'

Herbert had slapped his book shut and was struggling to his feet. His father untangled his newspaper and shook it into shape in front of him. Lily sighed and picked up her darning again. Herbert stumbled his way to the door and went out, banging the door shut behind him.

Lily looked at the barrier of newsprint in front of her husband's face. 'If it's any consolation,' she said wearily, 'I don't think Ethel's goin' to stop here much longer.'

The paper was lowered a couple of inches, revealing his eyes. 'Oh? What makes you think that?'

Lily shrugged. 'It's just a feelin' I've got.'

Something the signs told her, she thought, wielding her needle. Ethel had begun to behave differently, as if she had grown the muscles to be a separate person, somebody with an independent life. It was hard to pin down.

'Well, we've done our bit by her,' George said prissily, raising the paper again. 'Nobody can say we didn't.'

Lily bit her lip and concentrated on making the heel of George's sock respectable again.

\* \* \*

There were a lot of Americans in *The Wheatsheaf* that night. They were mostly in uniform, although a few were sporting bright jackets and bow ties, making themselves stand out from the locals like peacocks in a yard full of sparrows. The air was thick with mingling aromas of cigarette, pipe and cigar smoke overlaid on cheap perfume and sweat. At the piano two girls were squeaking the words of *I've Told Ev'ry Little Star* while a half-drunk GI banged out the approximate tune on the stained keys.

'Fridays get livelier all the time,' a barmaid said to Ethel. 'If this keeps up, we'll be makin' a profit again.'

Ethel nodded, eyeing her reflection in the mirror at the back of the bar. 'Nice crowd, an' all. Cheery.'

'It's the watery beer does it, love. They'd have to sink a few gallons apiece before they got fightin' drunk.'

Ethel wasn't drinking the beer. She had downed three small rums and now she was starting on a milk stout. She would have stayed on the rum but it was stuff that the Yanks had given the landlord, and it tasted funny. She would have a couple of stouts then maybe try a whisky or two, if they had any.

'Well hi.'

She turned awkwardly on her stool and saw Fat Aldo, an American sergeant who was usually too far gone by this time to talk to anybody. His regular drill was to put away as much drink as he could in the first hour, then sit in a corner and weep silently over his snapshots. Tonight, although he had been drinking, he looked far from sad.

'Hi,' Ethel said brightly.

'You're looking good tonight, honey.' Her gave her a playful squeeze. 'Can I buy you a drink?'

'Well . . .' She had been hoping that Bennie would be in by now. Bennie was her special chap; because of the nature of their relationship, she hesitated to call him her boyfriend. 'I was waiting for a friend . . .'

'Have a drink while you're waiting.'

'I'll have another one of these then, thanks.'

Most of the time the Americans were out to enjoy themselves in the pub. The more serious ones, the men who wanted to get off with a girl, went to Rainbow Corner, a US Forces social club, or to one of the little downstairs cabaret-bars dotted about the West End. Around Hackney it was beer, sing-songs and giggles, with only the occasional spontaneous pairing or serious relationship developing. The way Aldo was looking at Ethel, she felt he might have something more than a giggle and a song in mind.

'I've been watching you for a while,' he confided as the drinks were brought.

'I thought you'd just got here.'

'No . . .' He shook his head, making his heavy cheeks wobble and his collar badges glint. 'I mean, for a few days, when I've seen you in here.'

'Oh.' Ethel accepted the information without visible response. She sipped her stout and looked about her. 'The place is really filling up now.'

'You look lonely.'

She smiled at Aldo. 'You can't get lonely in here. I mean, look at it.'

'A girl can get lonely in the biggest crowd,' he said soulfully, edging closer until his stomach was prodding her arm. 'So can a guy.'

She frowned thoughtfully, putting floury grooves in her face powder. 'I've seen you lookin' a bit lonely now an' then, I must say. It's the wife an' kids, isn't it? You miss them a lot.'

'Yeah, well . . .' He ran a finger round the tight edge of his collar. 'What I'm saying, I guess, is nobody needs to be lonely. People can be friends, they can give each other warmth and take the pain out of each other's loneliness.'

His line was very direct, Ethel thought. No build-up to

talk of. She had been propositioned a time or two before and she could make comparisons. Some men came at her very slowly, talking about the weather, the rationing, the quality or the shortage of the beer. Aldo must really be wanting her, getting to the point as quickly as that. She felt sorry for him, in a way; men could be tempted so easily by a smart-looking girl, without her even trying.

'What say we have another drink here, then we can get a cab and go out on the town for a while?'

'Oh, I don't know, love . . .' What spoiled his approach, she thought, was his seriousness. He was too tense, he looked far too sombre. Ethel came out at night to enjoy herself. She couldn't imagine having many laughs with Fat Aldo.

'Come on,' he urged her. 'I can show you a real good time.'

She'd heard somebody say that in a film. 'It's nice of you, but I just want to sit here an' chat to a few friends an' things like that . . .'

Aldo's face was an open book. The words were simple, and in very large type. He was, in the words of Jim the landlord, lusting after a bit of rumpo. It didn't occur to Ethel, even though she read him clearly enough, that Aldo's attempt to win her over could be a desperate last resort. She imagined, rather, that her feminine appeal was throwing his senses into chaos. He was trapped by her allure, she believed, but she wasn't a girl to take advantage of that. She would let him down lightly.

'You're a nice chap, Aldo, but I've promised I'll meet a gentleman friend here . . .' As she spoke she saw little Bennie's head bobbing among the shoulders around the bar. 'Oh, there he is now.'

Aldo turned to see Bennie waving. 'Him?' Flushed and peevish he swivelled his head and stared at Ethel. '*Him*? That's the gentleman friend?'

'Yes . . .' Ethel was waving back.

'What in hell can a pipsqueak like that do for you?' Aldo made an angry grin. 'Christ. He isn't tall enough to lick a skunk on the ass . . .'

'Oh, he's very nice,' Ethel said defensively. 'Bennie's a gem when you get to know him.'

'Uhuh.' Aldo looked again, then shook his head in elaborate disbelief. 'I've seen some creepy set-ups in my time . . .'

'Whatever do you mean?'

'What's his trick? Does he grease his head, maybe, and use it like – '

A hand landed heavily on Aldo's shoulder. He spun around and saw the landlord staring straight into his face. 'Mind your mouth,' Jim snarled.

'What're you talking about?' Aldo's expression had become entirely innocent and bewildered.

'I was listenin'. If you want to start talkin' like that, go down the *Dog an' Fiddle* an' do it. Don't come in here foul-mouthin' my customers.'

By now Bennie was standing beside Ethel's stool. He was frowning at Aldo out of curiosity, but Aldo chose to misunderstand.

'Keep looking at me like that, pint-size, and I'll cram your skull through one of your buttonholes . . .'

'Right,' Jim said. He put down the empty glasses he had gathered and curled his fingers under the collar of Aldo's tunic. He marched smartly to the door, dragging Aldo with him, backwards. Other GIs began to laugh. None of them liked Aldo much.

'Let me go, you sonofabitch bastard! Take your Limey paws off!' At the door, holding the jamb with one chubby hand, Aldo glared across at Ethel and spat. 'Forget anything I said, bimbo! I'll tell a dog anything when I'm drunk!' A second later he disappeared as Jim pulled him out on to the street.

When the commotion had died away Bennie got himself

a drink and dragged a stool over beside Ethel's. Perched on top, he was scarcely an inch taller than her. His frizzy hair probably accounted for the height difference, she believed. He raised his half pint of beer in the gesture of a toast and sipped. Ethel watched him wrinkle his small nose as he swallowed; she suspected he came into the pub for the company, not for the drink.

'You mustn't let people like him upset you,' he told Ethel. 'Even if they call you names . . .'

'Oh, he didn't upset me at all.'

It was true. Aldo was just a big silly lump. He had got mad, Ethel knew, because his designs on her had been foiled. He was just another man who had to go away with his passions unspent, and they always behaved badly when that happened. She would have hated to be a man.

'What kind of day have you had?' she asked Bennie. This was how their conversations always went. They would tell each other about their day, then some feature of their recent experience – his or hers – would furnish the material for further talk. 'Did you get that book you were after?'

'No. The shortage has meant that people are buyin' up all sorts of books they usually wouldn't bother with – just to have somethin' to read. That means a particular one's harder to find.'

'Shame.'

'Yes, it is. Still, I have hopes, Ethel.'

He went on to tell her that his project, which was to write a study of the life of Karl Marx, wasn't being held back. He could work on certain parts and leave the others until he had his research material. The whole scheme impressed Ethel tremendously. She couldn't imagine being able to sit down and write something as long as a book. Letters were a problem for her; one page was usually as much as she could manage without getting a headache.

'And how's work?' she asked. 'Still got little problems?'

'Oh yes. The boss still thinks he's entitled to twice as much sweat out of me for no increase in wages. Typical capitalist.' Bennie swept up in a warehouse, a job he had done for so long, and for so many different employers, that he had become an authority. 'It's not just a matter of shovin' a broom about the place. There's a technique to it, Ethel. A positive skill, I'd go so far as to say. But the boss just wants me to move faster and sweep harder. It soothes the likes of him to see the proletariat under the yoke.'

She loved the big words he sometimes used. She was never sure what they meant, but she felt flattered to be treated as if she did. 'I've not had a very good day myself,' she said. 'Mrs Dollimore's been on my top again.'

'She sounds like a bit of a face-grinder herself.'

'I've explained to her I can't do buttonhole stitch. I mean, all I've ever learned was puttin' on buttons and buckles. She says I should do me share of buttonholes like the rest of them. I'm tryin' to learn, but it's not easy.'

There was a pause then: it would have been awkward, if it hadn't been for all the singing and talking and laughter around them. Finally Bennie cleared his throat and said, 'Have you given any more thought to what we talked about?'

Ethel glanced aside, fluttering her eyelashes. 'Well, yes, I have.'

'And?'

'I'd like to think about it a bit more, Bennie. I mean I like the idea but it's a big step, isn't it? Especially when we're not, you know, married . . .'

'Marriage is an outmoded bourgeois custom . . .'

'I know, you told me that.' She would have liked to know what bourgeois meant, but she was pretty sure she got his drift. 'Livin' together would be lovely, I'm sure. I know we respect each other enough, an' as you said it'd be like brother an' sister . . .'

'The companionship of two minds,' Bennie said gravely.

'Mm. But I need to be absolutely sure. You do understand, don't you?'

'I admire the fact you're takin' so long to decide,' Bennie assured her. 'It shows you're not shallow or impulsive.'

'We'll talk about it some time next week, eh?'

'If that's the way you want it, Ethel.'

Later, as Bennie saw her to the corner of her street, she wondered for the hundredth time why she held back. It would mean having a place where she didn't feel like a half-welcome lodger all the time. She would be content. Bennie was the kindest soul she'd ever known. They got on well together, even though he was a lot cleverer than her. And he wasn't after what most men were after.

Maybe that was it. Somehow, she couldn't imagine living with a man and sleeping in a separate room. That was how Bennie wanted it. None of the other, just companionship.

At the corner she turned and looked at him. He was so compact and cuddly, she thought. She wouldn't have minded curling up with him. But he'd have none of that.

'Goodnight then, Bennie. Thanks for seeing me home.'

''Night, Ethel. See you tomorrow night, will I?'

'Very likely.' He stood motionless as she placed a swift peck on his cheek. She stepped back and waved, then turned off along the street.

It was an odd old world, she thought. Here she was, going out every night to avoid staying in a house where there was an atmosphere, however hard Aunt Lily tried to cover it up. She went out dressed to kill, as she'd heard somebody put it, but she didn't really want men flocking round her. She wanted a little admiration and

35

she wanted companionship, the real kind, and that's what Bennie offered her. But she didn't know if she wanted that without . . . Oh, it was all so confusing.

She glanced up at the house as she neared the gate. At his bedroom window she saw Herbert, his shape visible in the dim glow from the fireplace behind him. The very silhouette was enough to make her heart sink. She felt the malice coming off him, the resentment and spite. It brought back the uncertain, abandoned feeling she'd worked so hard to smother.

As she pushed open the gate she looked back along the dark street and wondered. Maybe she should just say yes to Bennie and have done with it. It would please him no end, and it would take the strain off her.

# 4

On Christmas Eve the uniform workshops had an afternoon party. Only a modest affair had been planned, with a few sandwiches, cakes and some drink saved up over the year. By half-past four, however, it was clear that the small individual contributions added up to a glut of food and alcohol.

'We've been at it since half-three,' Aggie Cummins said, marvelling at the heavy-laden drinks table. 'There's enough left to see us through another hour at least.'

'Well, just make sure nobody overdoes anything,' Mrs Dollimore warned her. As manageress, she saw it as her duty to maintain proper behaviour in the workshop as well as an efficient work-flow. Moral decay, she knew, was rampant in London's wartime society; the least a trusted administrator could do was make sure it was curtailed within the bounds of her dominion. 'They're a bit silly, some of these girls. A lot of the men aren't much better.'

Aggie nodded and moved away, trying to emulate Mrs Dollimore's austere-faced authority. She had been chargehand in the sewing shop for nearly six months and she wanted to keep the job. The trouble was, nobody took her seriously. She didn't have the hard Dollimore eye, nor the acid tongue. She lacked height and width, too; Aggie was only five-foot-two and slim, an unconvincing lieutenant to a balloon-busted leader who topped five-ten. To make matters worse, Aggie was pretty.

'How about a Christmas kiss?' Dan Leach, grizzled and semi-toothless, had been rendered bold by more drink in one hour than he normally consumed in a month.

He came weaving towards Aggie with a curly sandwich in one hand and a whisky glass in the other.

'Sit down before you fall down,' Aggie told him.

'Aw, don't be like that, love. Just a little one. Come on . . .'

'I'd sooner kiss a scabby-headed pigmy.'

Aggie shouldered past him and crossed to the card table with the gramophone set up on it. One of the younger girls had been put in charge of the music, but she had wandered off long ago to join one of the giggling, merrymaking groups scattered about the room. Now people were shuffling through the records and putting on anything they wanted.

'What's that racket?' Aggie asked a girl who had just put on her selection.

'*Brother Can You Spare a Dime*. It's Bing Crosby.'

'It's a bit mournful, isn't it?'

'I suppose it is. But it's very touchin'. Suits Christmas, somehow.' The girl knuckled a dewy eye. 'It makes me bubble every time I hear it. Puts me in sort of a happy-sad mood.'

'I suppose the booze has helped your mood.'

The girl smiled wanly. 'I've had a few,' she admitted, watching the record spin.

They'd all had a few, Aggie thought as she wandered away. All except her. She had restricted herself to a couple of glasses of ruby port. She didn't want her authority to slip, not with Mrs Dollimore watching. Seeing the workers cavort and mingle, she wished the manageress would go home. It wasn't nice to be more sober than practically anyone else in the room.

'Oh, Lord . . .'

Over in a corner, half obscured by two rows of army greatcoats, she spotted Ethel Trent and a couple of the men. From the look of it, the Christmas spirit was overspilling into the territory of orgy. Ethel was against the wall, being hugged and mauled by both men. She was giggling and happily submitting to the feverish kisses they planted on her face and neck.

'Right then, come on . . .' Aggie pushed her way through the coats and grabbed one of the men by the sleeve. 'Pack it in, Romeo.'

The man was Andrew Clark, a van driver. He glared blearily at Aggie. 'Bugger off.'

'Yeah, bugger off,' the other man said, still clinging to the glassy-eyed Ethel.

'If you want to hang on to your jobs you'll pack it in right now.' Aggie grabbed the other man as the first one lunged at Ethel again. 'Chuck it, will you!'

Ethel slipped suddenly, her foot giving on a paper cake-cup. Aggie caught her by the armpits and pressed her firmly to the wall. Andrew Clark took the opportunity to run an exploratory hand across Aggie's seat. The shock made her bring back her elbow abruptly, catching him in the solar plexus. Andrew gurgled and turned aside, clutching himself.

'Aw,' Ethel whined, 'don't do that . . .'

'Listen! Ethel!' Aggie shook her, trying to bring her sense of proportion to the surface 'If Mrs Dollimore catches you – '

'I'm not doin' nothin'.'

'You were on the verge of doin' quite a bit, my girl.'

'I was just bein' nice to the chaps. It's Christmas, after all . . .'

Both men were huffily withdrawing. They had spotted Mrs Dollimore approaching, her head cocked quizzically.

'We was just enjoyin' ourselves,' Ethel complained. She stood away from the wall and swayed as Aggie released her. 'No harm in that.'

Mrs Dollimore came forward. She glared at the two men, then at Ethel. The conclusion she drew was swift and visible. 'What's the trouble?' she asked Aggie.

'She's got a bit tiddly, that's all.'

'Indeed.'

Ethel was trying to stand straight and look innocent in the intimidating presence. Her hair, originally styled in a series of interwoven curls copied from a magazine picture of Claudette Colbert, had collapsed into an irregular assortment of wavy strands. Two particularly long coils hung down over her left eye, making her look even more drunk than she was.

'And what do you have to say for yourself?'

'Just enjoyin' the party, Mrs Dollimore.'

The manageress took a step back, making a slow, sour-mouthed appraisal. 'You're a disgrace. What would your family think if they saw you like this?'

Ethel's concept of family was vague nowadays, even vaguer when she had taken a drink or two. She frowned and swayed again. Aggie reached forward and took her half-empty glass. Ethel had somehow managed to hang on to it while she was entangled with the two men.

'Listen to me, and listen carefully.' Mrs Dollimore folded her hands in front of her. To Ethel she looked like a big blotch of malice, ready to land anywhere she chose. 'As an employee you're a great disappointment to me.'

Ethel moved her tongue across her palate, preparing a defence. She was too slow.

'Your timekeeping is poor. The quality of your work is passable, but you're slower than anyone else – much slower, even though you've had plenty of practice.'

'Yes, Mrs Dollimore.' Ethel pushed back the strands of hair, which promptly fell over her eye again.

'Worst of all is your general conduct. You treat your responsibilities as if they were a game. You take nothing seriously. You're woolly. Irresponsible.'

Ethel nodded, waiting for the dark warning that inevitably followed the summary of her shortcomings. She had been through all this before.

'It comes as no surprise to me that you display moral laxity, or that you over-indulge in drink.'

'Maybe it's just because of the season,' Aggie mumbled, unable to leave Ethel completely undefended.

Mrs Dollimore ignored her. 'I've no wish to spoil anyone's enjoyment, but I believe you've gone far beyond the limits of anything that could be called enjoyment. Go to the washroom, tidy yourself up, and go home. If there's any repetition of this disgraceful behaviour, even a hint of it, you'll be dismissed.'

The next few minutes were confusing. In the cold air of the washroom Ethel began to feel very dizzy. She was aware that Aggie was helping her, pinning up her hair, dabbing cold water on her cheeks and forehead and telling her what a silly ass she was.

When she had managed to bundle Ethel into her coat Aggie stared closely at her. 'You're like a sheet. Are you goin' to be all right?'

Ethel nodded. It was unconvincing.

'Do you want to push two fingers down your throat, get it all up?'

'I won't be sick.' Ethel turned and looked at herself in the mirror. She did seem a bit white. But all she felt was wobbly. Not sick. These days drink hardly ever made her sick. 'I'll see meself out the back way.'

After more confusion – jerky movement, changing light, colder air and the uncomfortable guidance of Aggie's hands on her shoulders, Ethel found herself walking along a familiar road that would eventually lead her back to the house. The pavements were busy. People were talking louder than usual, and she was sure one or two waved to her. A few definitely gave her funny looks.

She tried to recall what had happened. It was rotten of old Dollimore to spoil things the way she did. Rotten of her and Aggie, really, except Aggie wasn't vicious like the Old Ma Dollimore. The men had only been messing about. It was what people did at Christmas; there was nothing in it. People just had nasty minds, Ethel decided. There was no changing them.

She stopped at the gate, taking deep breaths. With any luck she would get inside and up the stairs without meeting anybody. The walk in the fresh air had made her feel a lot steadier. She looked up at the darkening sky. About half-four, she supposed. When she got in she would set her alarm for seven and get into bed for a couple of hours. Then it would be up again and into the bathtub.

The prospect brightened her. A day that ended well could cancel all the upsets and annoyances that had gone before. And today was bound to end well. She was going to another Christmas party. Not only that. After too much hanging back and changes of heart, she was finally going to tell Bennie that she would move in with him in the New Year.

Ethel pushed open the gate and strode along the path. The house was easier to face, now she knew she wouldn't be staying there much longer.


'Man overboard!' somebody yelled. Sid the dustman had come off a table and hit the floor with a terrible thump. He had been standing there belting out *Pennies From Heaven* when he skidded over the edge and went down clutching his pint. The crowd cleared a swift circle around the spot where he had landed. Sid was on his back but still trying to sing, even though he was audibly winded.

Jim, the landlord, pushed his way forward and surveyed the situation. 'Leave him where he is,' he grunted. 'He's safer there.'

At the bar there was another bump, louder this time, accompanied by the sound of breaking glass. A girl, being carried on the shoulders of a young man, had leaned back and fallen, bowling over another couple of customers as she went.

'Hitler got it all wrong,' Jim remarked to someone standing nearby. 'He should have dropped a few million gallons of beer on us, then just let us wipe each other out.'

There were almost a hundred people in *The Wheatsheaf*. Although it had been announced that there would be a party that night, the gathering was less unified than the management had planned. Something like eight separate parties were going on, each with its individual brand of celebration, from group sing-songs and drinking contests to cheek-to-cheek dancing and the sentimental warbling of pre-war ballads. To Ethel, it seemed that she and Bennie were the only couple not connected to any group. She was reluctant to blame Bennie for that, although she had heard the rumblings.

'Miserable little bugger,' someone had observed. 'Can't get a smile out of him. He's sulkin' over there like a bear with mumps.'

It was true that Bennie had been gloomy all night. Ethel put his frequent moods down to all the reading he did, plus the fact that people didn't take to him much. She was sure they didn't want to listen to a lot of lectures about politics – especially coming from a man who swept floors for his living.

One punter had put the general feeling succinctly, after Bennie had informed him – without being invited to – that history was a natural process rooted in man's material needs. The man had leaned close and murmured, 'Why don't you shove your head up your arse an' see if it fits?'

Lately, Bennie's gloom had been preceding him into the bar. Ethel could see it coming and always tried her best to cheer him up. Sometimes it worked; tonight, though, there didn't seem to be a hope.

'You got a headache, Bennie? Maybe Jim's got somethin' behind the bar – '

'I'm fine, Ethel. Don't fuss.'

'I just thought – well, you seem that miserable . . .'

'Christmas isn't a time I enjoy. I never did.'

Ethel hadn't told him her decision yet. She had imagined them laughing and enjoying themselves when she sprang it on him, making him happier still.

'People can be such a pain, at times.' He sipped his drink without relish and bumped the glass down on the bar.

'They're just havin' fun.'

Ethel had a vague recollection of defending her own fun-making earlier that day. Bennie's stern rejection of the celebrations seemed to mirror Mrs Dollimore's grumpy attitude; thinking about it harder, Ethel decided he was behaving more like Cousin Herbert.

'At a time like this,' he suddenly intoned, 'fun isn't appropriate, Ethel. There's a war on. People are dyin'. Right now.'

'There's nothin' anybody here can do to stop that,' she pointed out. 'It's good for folk to let their hair down a bit . . .'

'Mindless, that's what it is. I'd bet that if – '

'Well, well,' a big, brawny man interrupted, slapping Bennie on the arm. 'A real dark one, aren't you?' He waggled his head at Ethel. 'Didn't say nothin' about there bein' a little lady in the picture.' He showed Ethel a wide, craggy-toothed grin. 'I'm Gilbert.'

'Ethel,' she said, letting him squash her hand. Bennie, she noticed, had turned a shade more grim.

'I work at the same place as Bennie here,' Gilbert said. 'Shop foreman,' he added grandly.

'Sounds interestin',' Ethel chirped.

'I must say it can be, Ethel.'

She could see he was giving her the once-over, taking

in her flared orange skirt, the low-necked pink blouse and the big gold-plated locket she saved for special occasions. Her hair was back in its Claudette Colbert style and she had made a careful job of her lipstick and rouge. Gilbert was impressed, she was sure. Bennie, on the other hand, hadn't seemed to notice how she looked.

'Takin' a rest from all that studyin' durin' the holidays, Bennie?'

Bennie's face stiffened. 'Why should I do that?'

'Just wondered.' Gilbert turned to Ethel. 'Always readin', he is. Every break-time there he is, book in front of him, notebook an' pencil at the ready. He'll make somethin' of himself, eh, Bennie?' The remark wasn't simply patronizing; it was voiced with an edge of light amusement that suggested Bennie would never get anywhere.

'I'm tryin',' Bennie said.

'Don't know how he does it, Ethel. My head would split with all that learnin'. It's always the same bloke he reads, an' all. Who is it again, Bennie? Harpo Marx or somebody . . .'

Bennie turned smartly and strode off to the toilet.

'I think he's in a bit of a mood,' Ethel explained.

'Always is.' Gilbert's tone had changed. Now that Bennie was gone he was frowning like a concerned uncle. 'He's gone sour with too much politickin', Ethel. If that workers'-promised-land he keeps on about is as miserable as he is, I don't want any of it. Not a bit.'

'He can be very cheerful at times,' Ethel tried lamely.

'With you, maybe. That'll be a front, if you'll pardon me sayin' so. A tactic to win you round.'

In spite of what a lot of people thought, Ethel reckoned she didn't miss a lot. It was common practice, she knew, for a man to poach. Part of the technique was to tell the girl what a dope her boyfriend was. It was done with an air of friendly counsel, as if the poacher – with the cleanest motives in the world – were saving her from making a bad mistake. But even knowing that, she was drawn to this beefy interloper. He was easygoing, there was no great intensity in him and he had a grin that warmed her. He didn't take life too seriously. Bennie, for his part, had begun seeing tragedy in everything. He detected what he called 'social sickness' in the simplest act.

'Do you fancy havin' a dance, Ethel?'

'Oh, well . . .'

'You could use a spot of cheerin' up, I reckon.'

She took a gulp of her rum. 'Why not?' Sliding from the stool, she noticed how strong Gilbert's grip was on her waist.

The tune, played on a tin whistle, was *Knees Up Mother Brown*, to which most of the nearby dancers were performing something like a polka. Gilbert took Ethel by the shoulders, obliging her to hold the bulge that passed for his middle. They slid into the churning throng like cars joining a major roadway, colliding a couple of times with other dancers until they were into the rhythmic flow around the ten-foot space by the door.

As she reeled and whooped and jumped to keep up with the whirling Gilbert, Ethel found she was conscious of two things at once. There was this, the sheer fun, the throat-hurting squealing and laughter as they cavorted about the floor, and there was the other matter, the reason why Bennie was so miserable.

'Enjoyin' yourself, Ethel?' Gilbert roared in her face.

'Ooh, yes!'

The trouble, she was sure, had to do with their last meeting. Bennie had raised the subject of them living together and, yet again, she had pleaded that she needed more time to think. By then she had known the exact reason for her hesitation. It *was* to do with their living like brother and sister. Not that she was sex-crazy. Far from it. Sex was all right but too many men got desperately serious about it. They got broody and possessive. What worried her about Bennie's proposition was that it went too far the other way. She liked a cuddle. She loved it, the holding of another person, the sense that she wasn't one lonely soul sharing a space with another one. Holding was a joining as strong as any other. But Bennie had made it clear there would be none of that.

'Come on, Ethel!' Gilbert yelled. 'Let's do it proper!'

Three other couples were doing a knees-up, their elbows linked as they attempted – or so it seemed – to land the odd kick on the ceiling.

'You'll have to hang on to me!' she howled back. 'I'll fall over, else!'

Even now, exerting every muscle, hearing herself laugh helplessly, the thought nagged her. He wanted her company, but he didn't want to touch it. That was odd. Earlier, that very morning, she had caught Uncle George's scowl over his paper. She had seen Herbert glaring openly at her on the stairs and she had thought, *damn it, I'm going*. But now . . .

The whistle-player increased the tempo.

'Hang on, Ethel!'

'Oh! Blimey! Help!'

There had been a bad few moments at their last meeting when Bennie had asked her, right out, how many men there had been. She'd asked what he meant. He had blushed in a not-very-pleasant way. 'Intimately,' he had said, coughing. 'Have there been many you've known that way?'

Ethel couldn't really say. There had been some, certainly, starting back in a woodshed in Camden Town when she was about sixteen, then once or twice in airraid shelters and in dark alleys after dances. None of that mattered – nobody had taken anything from her, as she saw it. It was something they did. Sometimes she enjoyed

47

it, other times she didn't. She told Bennie that. He had looked very glum.

'Keep this up,' Gilbert panted, 'an' I reckon I'll see in the New Year through an oxygen tent!'

Ethel was laughing too hard to say anything.

'You're a girl who knows how to enjoy herself – I'll say that for you!'

Ten feet away, Bennie stood staring, aghast. There she was, his lady friend, surrounded by clapping revellers as she energetically hoisted her knees, exposing her knickers for all to see. He watched for as long as he could bear, then he turned on his heel and marched out through the door. At that instant Ethel saw him. She saw the finality in his stride.

She leaned her head towards Gilbert. 'Bennie's gone!' she shouted.

'Sod him!'

'But maybe I should – '

'Forget Bennie the Broom!' Gilbert screeched, purple in the face and grinning so hard she could see his back teeth. 'Enjoy yourself!'

The drink and the strong arm around her and the enclosing warmth of this mad dancing and laughing – it was seductive and enthralling enough to make her let out a loud whoop and link arms with the girl dancing next to them.

'Oh, Lor' love us!'

At the back of her mind, though, there was something nagging. As the dancing stopped and she staggered with Gilbert towards the bar, she remembered that she had told her aunt, before she came out, that she would be leaving soon. For all her affection and sympathy, Lily had looked relieved. What was Ethel to do now?

Gilbert turned from ordering the drinks and grabbed her. 'Give us a kiss, Ethel!'

As she fell into his arms she set the newborn worry aside. It wouldn't go away, she knew that, but it could certainly be made to wait.

# 5

There were days of fleeting mist and endless, biting frost. The sky was sometimes silvery, more often a slow-shifting canopy of mottled grey above the drab, broken lines of city architecture. January had always been that way, as far as Ethel could recall. The war had merely added its own disfiguring measure to the bleakness and desolation. The note Bennie left at *The Wheatsheaf* might have been deliberately matched to the season – it was chilly, colourless, devoid of warmth or comfort.

*I will not see you again*, he wrote. *I realize now that I made a terrible mistake. Our friendship could never have survived your appetite for the coarser pleasures. I thought I had found a soul companion, but I was foolish and blind. I now know that your company, so freely given to whoever wants it, could hold no promise of anything fine or enduring.*

Ethel found the message pompous and strangely disturbing. She didn't feel that anybody had the right to judge her like that – certainly not Bennie, who knew nothing about her at all. After carrying the note in her handbag for a couple of days, she put it on the fire. Bennie could go to hell. She didn't miss him. What she missed, if she was honest, was the small hope he had held out, the prospect of change.

Things at the house had become worse. Even Aunt Lily had grown distant. She gave off an air of discomfort whenever she was near Ethel. One Saturday morning in the kitchen, after she had listened to the news and had learned that the Russians were smashing the Germans on nearly every European front, Lily switched off the wireless and turned to Ethel, who was drying the breakfast dishes.

'You told me, a while back, that you'd be leavin' soon . . .'

'Yes. I was goin' to move in at a friend's place, but – '

'I mean, you did say you were goin' – it wasn't a case of maybe . . .'

'No it wasn't. There was a snag came up, though – '

'Only I made arrangements, you see. About your room.' For the first time ever, Lily wasn't meeting Ethel's eyes. 'It's put me in a kind of awkward spot.' She lifted a towel, unfolded it, then began folding it again.

'Oh.' Ethel didn't know what to say. 'I could ask at work. There might be somebody that's got a place I could have . . .'

'It's not somethin' we can put off.' Lily was obviously embarrassed. She hung up the towel on the rail by the door and began stacking the dried dishes with frowning concentration. 'A promise is a promise, after all. Not that you actually promised, like, but it seemed pretty definite.'

'Yes. I'm sorry I didn't go when I said I would.'

Lily picked up the stack of dishes, then put them down again. She looked squarely at Ethel. 'I'm the one that should be sorry,' she said flatly. 'I'm ashamed of meself, Ethel.' She sighed, letting her eyes wander to the window. George was clearing the ground in his vegetable patches. 'We're a sorry apology for a family, an' that's a fact.'

Now it was Ethel who was uncomfortable. She wiped at a plate, swirling the water round and round, rubbing fiercely at the already spotless surface.

'It's got nothin' to do with me makin' arrangements about your room, love. I haven't made any at all.' She closed her eyes for a moment. 'Since our Wendy went away, I've had to take the brunt of it. All the moanin' an' groanin', the silences, the bad tempers. It didn't bother me that much, at first. But it's every day, Ethel. You could cut the atmosphere with a knife. It's wearin' me down . . .'

'I know,' Ethel murmured.

She hadn't known the precise reason, but she had wondered. The change in Lily's attitude had something to do with her, that had been plain enough. Ethel hadn't realized it had been the men making her aunt feel bad. Any way she looked at it, though, it was her fault. She wasn't wanted in that house. She should have got herself out of it long ago.

'I'm not one to go back on my promises, Ethel. I know what I said before – you're my kin an' you've got a home here. I'll not see you flung out or anythin' like that . . .'

'It'd be better if I went,' Ethel said quietly.

Lily was staring out of the window again, chewing her lip. 'It's not fair, I know . . .'

'I'll get somethin' arranged. Fast as I can.'

That afternoon, in her warm coat, woolly hat and thick gloves, Ethel went for a walk across the two acres of barren, rising ground that the locals called the park. She clambered over stony outcrops and hillocks, directionless, not caring where she trod. Her mind was as numb as the skin of her face. Confronted with the necessity of leaving, she felt paralyzed.

She walked slowly, watching her trudging feet through the misty trail of her breath. It had been a difficult couple of weeks since Christmas, knowing that her aunt was daily expecting her to announce that she was about to pack her bags. But that had been easy to live with compared to this. She was obliged to take action. She had to do something for herself, something that would need planning and a measure of will she didn't believe she possessed. How did people go about reorganizing their lives without help?

She stopped by an artificial pond, a miserable, unin-spired oval of water put there by the council before the war. The surface was dulled with grime and flaky patches of ice. Ethel watched as the wind bowed the clumps of weed and made tiny creases on the water's unwholesome skin. That terrible lonely feeling had come back, the feeling of being abandoned. She thought of her mother and father and felt the sharp sting of tears.

'You all right, love?'

She jerked round, startled. The young man was so heavily wrapped she could scarcely see his face. His cap was pulled down low on his forehead and his scarf almost met his nose.

'Yes, I'm fine.' She turned away again, dabbing at the tears.

'You looked like somebody thinkin' about jumpin' in.'

'No,' she said, keeping her back to him, trying to sound amused. 'I was just dreamin'.'

'A girl did jump in. A year or so ago.'

Ethel glanced at him. She could see now that he had a strong, friendly face. 'What happened?'

'It was so cold she scrambled out again, before anybody even got round to rescuin' her.' He came and stood beside Ethel. 'There used to be ducks here, you know.' .

'In a mucky old puddle like this?'

He nodded. 'They're not fussy, ducks. Specially when people keep comin' to feed them. I used to bring up some scraps for them meself, at weekends. They've all gone now, though. They say the bombin' scared them away to the outskirts.'

The image seemed very sharp to Ethel; the poor birds being dispossessed, driven out of their pond by the bombs and forced to make their home somewhere else. She sympathized.

'Live round here, do you?' he asked.

'Yes.' Ethel looked at him again. His eyes were light grey, surmounted by nice, straight, dark eyebrows. 'You from here yourself?'

He shook his head. 'I stay over Walford way. I come here Saturdays to see me sister. She's married to a Finchley chap. He's in the forces. She gets a bit lonesome on her own so I keep her company for an hour or two. Been doin' it for years.' He smiled, showing good strong teeth. 'Only thing is, she's out today. Left a note.'

'Oh.' Ethel found his tendency to chatter rather soothing. It distracted her. She couldn't think of anything to say herself, though. He would probably walk away in a moment.

'Dear oh dear.' He stamped his feet and dug his hands deeper into his coat pockets. 'It's a bit taters, isn't it? Fancy goin' for a cuppa? The caff down there's open.'

Ethel tried not to sound too grateful for the invitation. She trotted down the slope beside him, wondering where this little encounter would lead. She couldn't believe she had been picked up. It had been too friendly and a bit too quick for that; she hadn't detected anything but a simple sociable gesture. He was likely just a nice bloke, needing a bit of company. Like herself.

The tea they were served was a lot stronger than Ethel had expected. Wartime café brews were usually so weak you could scarcely taste anything but the powdered milk.

'It's always been a good place, this,' the young man said. When they sat down he had removed his cap. He looked younger at once, with a strong shock of dark brown hair that reminded Ethel of her father's. 'When my sister first came here to live, we used to be able to get a plate of sausage egg an' chips that would keep a hungry man goin' for a whole day. Smashin', it was.'

'It's certainly a nice cup of tea.' Ethel had taken off her hat and was patting her hair. She wished there was a mirror. She wished she had put on more make-up, too. 'It's funny, I live near here but I've never been in this place.'

'Been here all your life?'

She found herself spilling her whole story, or most of it, from the time when she had come home to find her parents, home and most of the avenue gone. She stopped short of telling him about her present troubles, although she mentioned how miserable her job sometimes made her.

'That's work for you. I'm a docker meself. There's times I'd like to chuck it in. Especially in this weather.' He paused with his cup halfway to his mouth. 'My name's William, by the way. William Skinner.'

'Ethel Trent.' She had been wondering what he was called. She had fancied he might be a Tom, or maybe a Peter. They were nice solid names that suited him. So did William, though.

'Don't think I'm bein' forward or anythin', Ethel. But I was wonderin'.' She had to wait until he'd taken a mouthful of tea. 'What do you do with yourself Saturday nights?'

'Oh. Not much, really.'

'I thought maybe you'd fancy a change of scene.'

'Where?'

'Over at Walford. I usually do a little tour of the pubs that've got music an' a decent beer ration.' His smile was faintly apologetic. 'But you might not like pubs . . .'

'Oh, I don't mind them.' There she went again, she thought; jumping at a chance to get her mind off a big problem that wouldn't go away, however hard she ignored it. The right thing for her to do that evening, she knew, was to meet up with some of the girls from work and find out if they knew of any cheap digs. But doing the right thing was always hardest; it was practically impossible when there was a strong alternative.

'I share a motor with one of the lads I work with,' William explained. 'It's my turn to have it tonight. I could pick you up an' drop you off again after.'

'That would be nice,' Ethel said. *A car!* she thought. She could hardly wait.

When the arrangements had been made – Ethel suggested he should pick her up on the corner of the street – and when they had finished their second cup of tea, they parted outside the café.

'Seven sharp, then,' William said.

'I'll be there.'

'Right.' He gave her his straight, honest smile. 'I think we'll have a good night, Ethel.'

She was sure they would. Of all the times she had agreed to go out with a young man, she couldn't remember it being so easy, so straightforward. He'd walked up to her, talked to her, bought her a cuppa and made a date. Just like that. William wasn't a flashy character, he wasn't the least bit pushy, yet he had a lot of confidence in himself. Ethel didn't believe he'd had any doubt that she would go out with him. She didn't think he would have any trouble giving her a good time, either.

Herbert watched her come down the stairs. She was decked out, he thought, like the classic whore. No one could accuse her of disguising what she was. As she reached the foot of the stairs he stepped out from the shadow of the parlour door. Ethel was startled. She knew that Lily and George had gone out to visit one of the people George nowadays called his colleagues. She had assumed Herbert had gone with them. But there he was, sneering as usual, hands stuffed in the pockets of his shabby brown cardigan.

'Off out on the streets again?' he enquired. He was always a lot bolder towards her when his parents weren't in the house.

Ethel went to the front door, trying to ignore him.

'The money must be good these days, with all those Americans about.'

Ethel turned the catch.

'I was talking to you,' Herbert snapped.

'An' I wasn't listenin'.'

'I don't know how you can live with yourself.' He said it as if there was bile in his throat. 'Don't you have any shame at all?'

Ethel's hand dropped away from the door catch. 'You've got no right to talk to me like that.'

'I'll talk to you any way I please. It's small compensation for being forced to live under the same roof with a tart.'

She looked at him. He wouldn't spoil the night for her. She wouldn't let him. What she should do, without hesitating, was walk out without letting him say another word. But Ethel wanted to hit back.

'You're a fine one to talk about anybody else,' she said.

Herbert's eyes shifted with momentary uncertainty. 'I beg your pardon?'

'You're always spoutin' the Bible an' stuff like that – but it's not always the Bible you're readin', is it?'

He swallowed audibly. 'I don't know what you're talking about.'

'All them books with the dirty pictures, that's what.'

Now he gulped, bringing up a warning finger. 'I won't stand here and be slandered by the likes of you, you – '

'Dirty pictures is for dirty little minds!'

'Dirt and filth are what *you* know about!' he shrieked. 'They're your element! If I choose to acquaint myself with what's evil, it's because I have to be forearmed! Know thine enemy!'

'You're the only enemy you've got, Herbert.'

On that note Ethel decided she had hit back enough and should remove herself. She opened the door smartly and went out, leaving Herbert red-faced and fuming in the hall.

Making her way to the corner, she reflected on the possible outcome of that exchange. He would be more careful with her in future, she supposed. Now he knew that Ethel was in on his nasty secret, he wouldn't risk having her say anything about it in front of his father or mother.

'Sweaty, dirty beast,' she grunted, walking carefully on the new high-heeled shoes. She had seen the books and pamphlets one afternoon when she had offered to do some polishing and dusting for Aunt Lily. They were strewn across the bottom of an open drawer. She knew Herbert always kept the tallboy drawers locked, she'd heard the key turning several times when she passed the room. That day he had gone out to the newsagents and forgotten to take the usual security measures. It was quite a collection. Ethel had flicked through them swiftly then left the room with a face like a beetroot.

She thought about Herbert again as she stood waiting for William to arrive. It was all very well that he would be cautious of her in future; the fact was that life in the house was a strain, for her and for Aunt Lily. It would be even harder now, with all that extra tension and malice in the atmosphere. She had to get out, as soon as ever she could. But for tonight, she prayed, she would be able to put it all from her mind.

She couldn't. As the evening wore on, as she was taken to place after place and introduced to nice people who granted her their geniality and their warmth, Ethel realized that she had a problem so big that, for once, it got in the way of her recreation.

Eventually, in a Walford pub called *The Queen Victoria*, on the corner of Bridge Street and Albert Square, William looked directly at her and said, 'You're not enjoyin' yourself, are you?'

'Of course I am.'

'No you're not, Ethel. I'm sorry about it, an' all. I

really thought, when I talked to you today, that you was the kind of girl could enjoy doin' the things I do. It was a mistake . . .'

She recalled Bennie's note: *I realize now that I made a terrible mistake.* Bennie had. William hadn't.

'It's . . .' She stared at her drink, swirled it, looked at him. 'I should be havin' the time of my life, William. Truth is, I've got a big problem an' it's playin' on me mind.'

'Then tell me about it.'

She explained. She left out nothing, not even the recent encounter with Herbert.

When she had finished William smiled at her. 'You've no more got a problem than I've got a hump on me back.'

'Pardon?'

'I can get you digs tomorrow – sooner, if it's that urgent.'

Ethel stared. 'Really?'

'I wouldn't joke about anythin' that's gettin' you down this bad. Look, my sister Edie's got two rooms goin' beggin'. Has had for months. She's been a bit chary about lettin' them out to strangers, even though she could use the extra and the company. One word from me, they're yours. How about that, Ethel? Your own little flat.'

She was still staring. 'You mean it?'

'Well of course I do.'

'That's – marvellous.' For the first time that evening she smiled without having to force herself. 'Marvellous!'

'I wish to God you'd told me earlier. I really thought it was me that was the trouble.'

She shook her head. 'You're no trouble at all, William.'

He grinned and leaned close. 'You mean you could get to like me?'

'I got to a while ago,' she told him. 'In that caff – halfway down me first cup of tea.'

# 6

A few weeks before she left school at the age of fourteen, Ethel had fallen over during a game in the playground. She struck her head on a cornerstone and passed into unconsciousness for several minutes. When she came round she complained of a bad headache, but otherwise she seemed unharmed.

In the ensuing months, however, her mother noticed a profound change in Ethel. She had never been the brightest child in creation, but she had always shown a certain doggedness in her approach to life's challenges. She had learned to knit and crochet by the time she was ten, she was an adequate cook and in the evenings she often had the patience to immerse herself in a good story book.

By the time she left school, she was displaying behaviour which puzzled her mother. 'She's like a grasshopper,' Mrs Trent told a neighbour. 'Can't seem to stick with anythin' for more than a minute before she's got to be at somethin' else.'

It wasn't merely impatience. Ethel lacked concentration. Her sense of order seemed to have fled her, too; her room at the top of the house became untidy, she mislaid things easily and didn't seem to care so much about her little hobbies.

After leaving school Ethel had three short-lived jobs. She worked first in a factory, where she had to mind a button-covering machine; after that she found a position as a junior sales assistant in a milliner's shop, then as a dish-washer in the kitchen of a London Transport canteen. She lost all three jobs because of her erratic work and bad timekeeping.

Finally, three years before the outbreak of war, when Ethel was sixteen, her mother managed to have her accepted by a domestic employment agency. She left home to take up work as an under-maid to a well-to-do family in Hackney. Stern supervision kept her in line and she held the post until 1940, when she returned home to do part-time war work, sewing on uniform buttons and buckles.

During those years Ethel maintained her own unspoken view of what had happened to her. That knock on the head, she believed, had sprung some hidden door in her brain.

On the day of the accident, although she complained of no more than a headache, she experienced something else that would have been hard to describe to another person. A number of things she saw and heard – a casual remark by her father, the chink of one cup against another as her mother moved them, the sight of the family cat jumping down from the window ledge – seemed to be pre-echoed in Ethel's mind. She felt sure she knew what was going to happen just before it actually did.

Alongside the change in her personality and behaviour, the strange foresight persisted, intermittently, throughout all the years that followed. Ethel never mentioned it to anybody. She believed it was a mysterious gift, granted by that accidental blow to her skull.

She had been living with William's sister, Edie, for two months when she began to wonder if her gift wasn't a lot deeper and more powerful than she had realized. It happened on a windy Friday evening when she came into the neat terraced house and found Edie in the kitchen, making the usual pot of tea.

'It'll be ready in a wink,' Edie said brightly.

Ethel took off her coat and sat down at the table, as she always did for ten minutes every day after work. She watched Edie moving about near the cooker. She was a tall, broad-faced, perpetually active woman in her thirties. She had no children and no wish for any, preferring to be a good housewife with plenty of free time to help other people. Something helpless in Ethel had drawn Edie to her the moment they met.

'The British have retaken Mandalay, Ethel. It was on the wireless a minute ago.'

'That's nice.'

'And there was that heavy air-raid on Berlin yesterday.' Edie sighed contentedly and jiggled the teapot to hurry the brew. 'One way an' another, this war's comin' to a quick end.'

'So they say.'

Ethel had been hearing about a swift end to the war for years. She had no particular faith in other people's optimism, but she never argued.

'It's in the cards, too,' Edie murmured, setting out the cups.

'Pardon?'

'I consulted the cards, Ethel. It's a talent I've got.' She averted her head with modest pride. 'It doesn't do to abuse it, you understand. The talent can leave you if you don't treat it as somethin' special. The news bein' the way it is, I thought it was special enough to have a peek into the future.'

Ethel felt her pulse quicken. She had always thought that card-reading and palmistry and the rest of that malarkey was the province of cranky old dears with too much time on their hands and not a lot in their heads. But Edie was a sensible, intelligent woman. A no-nonsense type. Ethel thought of her own weird little talent. Only the day before, she had known a clothing rack was going to fall over just a moment before it did.

'How did you learn?' she asked Edie.

'Learn?'

'How did you know you could read the cards?'

61

'Oh, it's so far back I can hardly remember. I suppose I just always knew I could see things that other people couldn't. Before I turned to the cards, I couldn't really control the talent. It came an' went, an' it never told me much of any importance.'

So maybe, Ethel thought, if she found something that could make her own gift more manageable, she could find out really useful things, important things, in advance.

'I think maybe I'm a bit like that, Edie. I can sometimes tell things before they happen.'

Edie poured the tea carefully. 'I think most folk think they can, love. You have to train a talent first, before you know if it's worth anythin'.' As she put the cups on the table she added, a little haughtily Ethel thought, that a true talent was very rare indeed.

'I suppose you're right.'

But Ethel wouldn't be put off. The idea of nurturing something special in herself, making it flower into a unique, mystical skill, was more intriguing than anything she could imagine. Later, as Edie was answering the door and putting off one of the numerous ladies who came in search of spare woollens and blankets. Ethel surrendered to an impulse.

Tea leaves, she thought. That was how a lot of them did it. You drained the cup, turned it upside down on the saucer and turned it two or three times. She had seen girls at work playing the game. Maybe it would be more than a game if somebody with a gift tried it. She gulped down the remains of her tea, upended the cup and twisted it on the saucer.

She looked at the mess inside. The trick was to let it register as a picture, like the faces that seemed to appear on wallpaper at odd times. Ethel stared. She saw something very much like a letter R. It was linked to what might be an O, just above it. Below, also linked, was a very rough P. Beneath that there was just a spatter of tea leaves, with a stunted vee-shape on top. She kept looking until she heard Edie coming back. She put the cup back on the saucer, firmly memorizing what she had seen; reading from roughly the top, it was ORP, then a vee-topped splodge. It wasn't as riveting a sign as she would have wanted, but she decided it was something. She would hang on to it and see if it truly meant anything.

A month later, Ethel was granted a blinding flash of revelation that proved, as far as she was concerned, that she possessed a true psychic talent.

Two days after she had carried out her experiment with the tea leaves, a V2 rocket had landed in the south-east of the city. The event hadn't cause much general interest, since well over a thousand of the rockets had already landed on Britain. By the middle of April, how-ever, expert observers were saying that the V2 explosion in March had probably been the last one of the war. Edie conveyed the news over the late-afternoon cup of tea, along with other snippets from the BBC.

Ethel registered the information slowly. Then it hit her with a jolt.

'Where did you say it was?'

'Where what was?'

'The rocket last month. The last one ever.'

'Orpington.'

Ethel was speechless. ORP, over a splatter with a V on top. What picture could be clearer? What omen could be more vivid?

A couple of minutes later she withdrew to her rooms on some vague excuse. She sat by the window for several minutes, staring at the blue-and-yellow marbled sky. This must be how saints felt, she thought, when they realized they were blessed. She had never felt more important in her life.

Now she had exercised the gift and knew its power, what changes could she make in her own life? She thought for a while, but only trivial things occurred; clothes, money, a big house. She realized she was getting it all wrong. She couldn't influence fate, she could only glimpse its workings in advance. So what did she need to know about her future?

'William an' me,' she whispered.

Every Saturday, since she had moved here, William had come over from Walford and taken her out. They were sound friends by now, enjoying the same things and always content in each other's company. He had already made the odd reference to deeper feelings: 'We've got somethin' special in common, Ethel. I hope we don't lose it.' She hoped so, too, because she believed she was in love with William.

So. She wanted to know how it would turn out between them. Loss was something she had come to expect. She didn't want to lose that young man, but even if it was fated to happen, she would sooner be warned.

She realized she had left her teacup downstairs. It would look odd if she went down and rescued it after all this time. She didn't want Edie to know that she, too, had the gift of seeing forward. It was a fact Ethel couldn't quite fathom; perhaps she feared jealous friction, or rivalry.

She thought of her friends at work again and remembered something. One of them was an Irish girl with a headful of remedies for just about everything – her acne, though, appeared to be beyond her healing powers. She was also very superstitious. She had once demonstrated a variation on the tea leaves technique, using coloured glass beads.

Ethel dug around in one of her trinket boxes and found three strings of beads that she could bring herself to sacrifice. One was red, one blue, the other green and black. With nail scissors she cut the strings and shook up the beads in her cupped hands. Conscious of the serious nature of the occasion, she stood over the bedspread, closed her eyes, thought of herself and William, then let the beads fall.

When she looked, all she saw was a jumble of colour. She kept on looking, letting her eyes slip out of focus. After a time a picture emerged. It was a ragged shape, but it was certainly there, and it became clearer the longer she stared. It was a figure eight. It was on its side, but she assumed an eight was an eight any way you looked at it.

Perhaps it meant eight years, she mused, as she gathered up the beads and dropped them into the trinket box. Or eight months. Eight days, perhaps? Was that what she was being told? They would be together for eight something? Not long at all, however it was measured. Still excited by the discovery of her ability, Ethel decided not to feel too bad. There could be another meaning. She doubted it, though.

That Saturday William took her to *The Queen Victoria*, the Walford pub where she had told him all about her problems, and where he had solved them for her. The place was buzzing with talk and laughter. Two soldiers from the neighbourhood had come home that week and a good consignment of beer had been delivered to the pub the day before. Both facts provided the ingredients for celebration. By the time Ethel and William arrived, people were already beginning to dance as the landlord, Gus Leonard, went round checking his blackout curtains.

'Looks like we'll have a right time of it here,' William observed, nodding to a few locals he knew. 'I reckon this is my favourite pub, Ethel.'

Ethel looked round, nodding. The interior was authentic, well-preserved Victorian. There was a wealth of dark polished wood, buttoned leather and etched glass. The lamps glowed in amber shades. 'I could get to like it a lot, meself.'

As they shoved their way to the bar William pointed to a couple sitting near the door. The woman was about thirty and enormously pregnant. The man beside her had been handsome once, Ethel could see, but he had a sickly pallor and the deep-set eyes that were the common legacy of prolonged illness.

'That's Lou and Albert Beale,' William said. 'He was a prisoner of the Japs for a while. Nice couple. I'll introduce you, after.'

Flo the landlady, took William's order. 'Stay close to the bar, love,' she said. 'One of the lads that came home this week brought a Gerry camera with him. He's goin' to take our picture. You might as well get in on it.'

During her first drink Ethel pretended to be engrossed in what was going on around her. In fact she was watching William, every chance she got, realizing how each movement of his head, every smiling twitch of his mouth had endeared itself to her. She did love him, she had no doubt of it now. It saddened her terribly to think they might fall out soon, or be separated for some other reason.

'Chin up, Ethel,' she muttered to herself firmly.

Her awesome power would keep her from despair; people like her, she fancied, must always have some special destiny. Things would have to work out for the best, but they must be allowed to work out without hindrance. She would have to be brave, that was all there was to it.

During the second and third drinks, as she met more people and joined in a chorus of *We'll Meet Again*, her mind wandered away from herself. She began to detect something different about people. They definitely believed the war was coming to an end. The staunch, come-what-may cheerfulness of the past few years was giving way to a genuine sheen of hope and a carefree spirit of celebration. Ethel believed the war was coming to an end, too. The last V2 had fallen, after all. She wouldn't have taken an expert's word for it – but the tea leaves were something else.

'Right then, you two, get in line.' The young soldier with the camera was shepherding people into a cluster at one end of the bar. 'We want big smiles and no eyes shut. Come on, then!'

The pregnant woman, Lou Beale, was reluctant to get in the picture.

'Not lookin' like this,' she complained. 'I'm like a bleedin' barrage balloon.'

'Come on, love,' the soldier coaxed her. 'It'll be a souvenir, won't it? You might not look like that again.'

'Not if I can help it!'

The soldier tapped Ethel's arm. 'Hold this a minute, will you?' He handed her the camera. 'I'll get this group tidied up if it kills me.'

As he fussed around, getting people to change places, tidying the lines of his composition, Ethel hefted the camera. 'It's really heavy,' she told William. 'Hope I don't drop it.'

'More than your life's worth, Ethel. Give it here.'

As William relieved her of the instrument Ethel noticed something. There was a series of markings on the barrel around the lens. One of them seemed to jump out at her.

'William . . .'

'What?'

Ethel pointed to the symbol. It was printed in stark white; it was a figure eight, but it was lying on its side. 'What's that mean?'

He shrugged. 'Search me. Cameras are a mystery, far as I'm concerned. I even get lost with the old Brownie.'

Ethel's heart was thumping. When the soldier came back to retrieve the camera she tugged his sleeve. 'What does that mean, love?'

67

He frowned at where she was pointing. 'They're the focusing distances.'

'But that one there.'

He peered closer, where the scarlet tip of her nail was touching the barrel. 'Oh. That means infinity.'

The rest of the evening was lost on her. Ethel sailed through the jollity in a state of bemused distraction. The word thrummed in her head. *Infinity*. She didn't know what it meant. She'd heard 'infinite' before, but she had only the haziest of notions what that meant. She wouldn't sleep until she knew. The shock of seeing the symbol was enough to keep her awake for a night or two anyway, she thought.

Before William left her that night he drew her close and kissed her. 'Smashin' night, Ethel.'

'As usual,' she said.

He looked at her. 'You're feelin' all right, aren't you?'

'Of course I am.'

'Only I thought you was a bit, well, distant at times.'

'It was all the excitement.'

He looked closer, not entirely convinced.

'Silly.' Ethel drew him to her and gave him a hug. On tiptoes she kissed him. 'See you next week, eh?'

'Next week,' he smiled. 'Without fail.'

When Ethel got indoors Edie was sitting by the wireless, listening to a late news bulletin. Ethel waited until the broadcast was over, then she came straight out with it.

'What does infinity mean, Edie?'

Edie blinked. 'What do you want to know that for?'

'I just heard the word tonight, that's all. It's been plaguin' me – you know how some words do.'

Edie stood up. 'Well, I'm not rightly sure. I can sort of guess, without puttin' it into other words . . .' She turned and reached down to the radio cabinet. There were some books on the shelf underneath. 'Let's have a look.' She

68

hoisted out an old, split-backed dictionary. 'Infinity,' she murmured, riffling. 'Infinity . . .' She flipped some more, then ran her finger down a page. 'Ah.' The finger stabbed and she peered closely at the page. '"Infinity. Endless time and space."' She closed the book and looked up. Ethel was staring, wide-eyed, her mouth half open. 'What's up?' Edie asked her.

Ethel swallowed. 'Nothin'. Nothin' at all.' She grinned at Edie and turned back towards the hall. 'Reckon I'll get an early night, then.'

'Don't you want a cuppa before you go up?'

'No, ta. I'm really wore out.' She went towards the stairs, waving absently. 'Good night, Edie.'

'Sleep tight, Ethel.'

'I will.'

She was still awake when the downstairs clock chimed two. The onrush of relief had followed her into bed, where it was swiftly supplanted by renewed shock and staggering realization. She could actually do it! She could see into the future! And what a future she had waiting for her. Nothing had ever equalled this. Nothing had come close. Now, sleepless as she was, Ethel felt safer and happier than she had in her entire life.

As sleep began to come a question nagged her, though not strongly enough to keep her awake; what was that symbol doing on a camera? Maybe it was a very special camera. The Germans, she'd heard, although they were a bunch of swine, were very clever people. Dead clever, if they made cameras that could take pictures of endless time and space.

Endless time and space! Now *there* was an omen to hang on to, a sign to cherish. Ethel hugged the pillow as sleep gently sucked her in. 'William, William,' she sighed, smiling. There couldn't be a happier girl in all London.

# 7

To emphasize the fact that only one war had ended and that another one was still being fought, the British Government decreed that 8 May 1945 was to be known as Victory in Europe Day. Most people knew that it was only a matter of time before the Japanese succumbed to the Allies' military pressure in the Philippines and in their homeland. It was all over. Peace had come.

'It's more like another bloody war's broke out,' a man in *The Wheatsheaf* bawled to Jim, the landlord. At midday there were more people in the pub than anyone had ever seen there at one time. Energetic pushing and shoving around the bar was accompanied by broad smiles and repeated apologies as men and women were bumped, elbowed, jostled and had their toes trodden. 'Reckon there'll be enough drink to go round, Jim?'

'Just about.' Jim winked as he served two customers at once. 'I've been savin' up. If we do run out, I'll start givin' them cold tea. The state they're in already, I doubt they'd notice the difference.'

Outside, a moveable street party was spilling over into gardens and back yards. Men in uniform, others in makeshift John Bull suits and others simply draped in flags danced with anyone they could grab, while wives set out plates of sandwiches and stodgy cakes on long trestle tables. Rings of children performed the little victory dances they had been learning at school for the past six months. Old men and women stood in doorways and at gates, nodding to the music from accordions, melodeons and banjos. There was noise, merriment, wild celebration. The sun shone.

Ethel was in *The Drayman's Arms*, a pub at the opposite end of the street from *The Wheatsheaf*. She hadn't been able to make it to her local; three attempts had been foiled by eager men with grasping hands who kept trying to draw her into the frantic kerbside revelries. Finally Ethel and her companion, Aggie Cummins, had settled for this place. It was small and cramped and the pair had to jam themselves into a corner by the rear window. Uncomfortable as they were, the drink was flowing as steadily as anywhere else, and so far the girls hadn't had to pay. People just kept handing them glasses.

'You'll never believe this,' Aggie said breathlessly, moving from her tight corner and wedging herself in on the other side of Ethel. 'That Nancy from the tailoring shop . . .'

'The one with the bad leg?'

Aggie nodded. 'She'll have more than a bad leg when this lot's over. I couldn't stand there another second.'

Ethel craned her neck to see through the window. The yard was stacked with crates and for a moment she couldn't see anybody. Then she spotted Nancy, leaning on a door, her arms and knees hugging a man in uniform. They moved against the planks of the door with a fast, urgent rhythm. Ethel smiled and looked at Aggie.

'She's just celebratin'.'

'I think it's awful.'

'It's human nature.' Ethel swallowed some of her drink. She wasn't sure what it was. It certainly wasn't beer, even though it looked like bitter. 'You have to make allowances, Aggie. It's a special event – likely the most special one we'll ever see.'

Aggie shrugged and stared across the bar, eradicating the startling image that had printed itself behind her eyes. Three weeks before, she had been demoted at work in favour of a more experienced woman. She was no longer a chargehand, and the loss of status had appeared to come as a relief. She began mixing freely with the other girls and had been pleased when Ethel had suggested they spend the day together.

'I suppose I'm just not used to bein' out among people.' Aggie watched three women offer an extravagant welcome to a young soldier who had just come in. One of them was actually licking his face. 'It's all so – abandoned, isn't it?'

'An' it's hardly started yet.'

A man leaned across and kissed Ethel on the cheek. She smiled at him. He smiled back, then moved away.

'Who's he?' Aggie asked.

'Never saw him in me life before.' Ethel grinned at her friend's shocked expression. 'Relax, Aggie. Just enjoy yourself.'

'I'll try.' Aggie sipped her drink, watching Ethel over the rim of the glass. After a moment she tilted her head at Ethel. 'I'll tell you somethin',' she said. 'I envy you. Does that surprise you?'

'More'n a bit. I always believed you thought I was a fallen woman.'

'I'm not sure what I thought. But you've a knack of gettin' people's friendship without tryin'. That's not easy. I can't do it. Especially with chaps. They either think I'm snooty or they take liberties.'

Recently, when she had decided she would like to be proper friends with Ethel, Aggie had explained that she lived with her widowed mother. It was a dry, boring existence. Most nights they sat indoors with the wireless for company. Attractive as she was, Aggie had only ever been out with three men. She was Ethel's age, twenty-five, and it had lately dawned on her that she might be destined for the shelf, unless she did something about it.

'Maybe you try too hard,' Ethel said. 'If you relax a bit, like I said, an' just let things happen, you won't go far wrong. You might get into the odd awkward scrape, but you'll get by – an' you'll not be short of friends.'

Aggie sighed. It was one thing to be told, another to do what you were told. She had kept herself back too long, she believed. She noticed that a man at the bar was staring. She looked away sharply.

Ethel had emptied her glass. 'We'll have another couple here, eh? Then we'll go over to Walford.'

'Are you sure your chap won't think I'm intrudin'?'

'Course he won't.' Although it was a national holiday, an emergency shipment had to be unloaded at the docks that morning. William was required to work for a few hours. Ethel had suggested that, just for once, she would go to Walford and meet him. 'You'll come across a lot of nice people over there, Aggie. They'll all be glad to see you.'

A few minutes later, after a short exchange with the landlord, Ethel learned that the stuff she had been drinking was cider. By that time, she knew that it was fairly potent. So did Aggie, even though she had been taking it slowly. As they pushed their way out to the street she clutched Ethel's arm. 'I don't want to get tiddly,' she said. 'I did that one time an' made a right fool of meself.'

'This is just the day to make a fool of yourself,' Ethel told her. 'Everybody else is doin' it. I'll see you don't get too far-gone.'

'Who's goin' to keep an eye on you?'

'William. He always knows when I've had enough.' Ethel squeezed her friend's arm. 'Do as you're told. *Relax*.'

At the corner they found an abandoned taxi. 'Wish I could drive,' Ethel said. 'I can't see the police bookin' anybody for stealin' transport on a day like this.'

They stood by the cab for five minutes. Finally the driver showed up. He came ambling along the pavement grinning and shaking his head, as if he was listening to an invisible man telling him a joke. His grin widened when he saw the girls in their summer frocks, leaning on his vehicle.

'I'm off duty, ladies. Just usin' the cab for personal purposes.' He glanced to right and left, moving closer. 'Tell you what, though. If you're goin' to a special party or anythin' like that, an' if you can get me invited, I'll take you there for nothin'.'

'We're goin' to the Queen Vic in Walford,' Ethel said. 'No special party goin' on, as far as I know. Just a party like the ones round here.'

He considered what she had said. 'That's the pub on the corner of Bridge Street an' Albert Square, right?'

'That's it.'

He exhaled a small cloud of warm, beery breath. 'Nice lookin' landlady, as I remember.' He shrugged. 'No harm tryin' me luck in another parish. Hop in, girls. The Queen Vic it is.'

They made slow progress. Street after street was closed for the celebrations, and those that were open were crowded with people and traffic. On the way Aggie became quiet for a time. When Ethel asked her what was wrong she was evasive for a minute, then admitted she was fretting about her future.

'Can't get it out of me head. Everythin's goin' to change. We'll be out of a job soon. What are you goin' to do?'

'I've been tryin' not to think about it,' Ethel said. 'What about you?'

'I want to get married an' have a family.' The drinks had made Aggie unusually direct. 'I always thought I'd settle down when peace came. But here it is an' here I am – I don't even have a fella.'

Ethel shrugged. 'I suppose there'll be plenty of extra

74

jobs from now on. An' spare blokes. You can work some place else while you're gettin' your plans made.'

Aggie listened and nodded, staring with the intensity of a not-too-sober person. 'Are you an' your William goin' to tie the knot?'

'Oh . . .' Ethel hesitated, then shook her head. 'Not yet, I don't think.' In spite of their deep involvement with each other, Ethel and William had never discussed marriage. She would have raised the matter, some way or other, if it hadn't been for something William had said to her. He had been talking about another couple at the time. 'I don't think people should rush into marriage,' he told Ethel. 'They ought to know each other a couple of years, at least, before they start makin' them kind of plans.'

'Maybe he's not the marryin' kind,' Aggie said.

'Maybe not,' Ethel murmured. But she would stay with him, whatever kind he was. It was destined, after all.

When the taxi drew up outside *The Queen Victoria* there was a riotous street party going on in Albert Square. The noise from the pub was nearly as loud as the din going on around the houses. When the girls had alighted the driver got out, grinning, the way he had been all the way across from Hackney. He nodded to Ethel, locked the cab doors and disappeared into the throng without saying a word.

Aggie was looking nervous again.

'Don't panic,' Ethel told her. 'They're all friendly.'

'But there's that many of them, Ethel. Look at it. I never saw such a crowd on the streets.'

Ethel was soothed by the chaos, the noise and the frantic movement. Involvement with people was crucial to any sense of happiness; to be involved with that celebration, all she had to do was be there. She watched, beaming, as a huge conga line of people weaved in and out of the crowds and around the flag-festooned lamp posts.

'That's your chap over there, isn't it?' Aggie was pointing towards a house at the corner of the square.

'Where?'

Ethel bobbed her head, trying to see past the people who were thronging the end of Bridge Street. Suddenly she saw William. He was by the gate to the house, speaking earnestly to a tall young man in a dark business suit.

'Who's that he's with?' Ethel asked Aggie.

'How should I know?'

'Looks like a lawyer or somethin'.'

Ethel took her friend by the arm and led her into the crowd. They shoved their way to where William was standing. His face lit when he saw her.

'Ethel!' He switched his smile and shared it with Aggie, whom he had met only once before. 'Enjoyin' yourselves?'

Both girls nodded. 'We've had a grand time so far,' Ethel said. 'Haven't we, Aggie?'

'Smashin'.'

'This is the local doctor,' William said with some pride. 'Dr Legg, this is my girlfriend, Ethel, an' her friend . . . ah, Aggie, isn't it?'

The doctor shook hands with both girls.

'We've been talkin' over a bit of business,' William explained.

'Nothin' wrong with you, is there?' Ethel searched William's face, as if she were looking for signs of disease.

'Nothin' like that,' he said. 'I'll tell you about it later.'

'I have to be going,' Dr Legg said. 'If I stay here any longer I won't want to go – and I'm overdue at my uncle's house as it is. He'll be wondering what's happened to me.'

William reached out and took his hand. 'Thanks again, Doctor. You've been a big help.'

'It was a pleasure. I hope everything works out the way you've planned.'

They all waved as Dr Legg moved off across the square.

'Posh, isn't he?' Ethel remarked.

'Salt of the earth, that bloke,' William assured her. He watched until Dr Legg had disappeared into the crowd, then he turned and pointed to the pub. 'Fancy battlin' your way through the mob an' havin' a jar, girls?'

By the time they reached the bar Aggie looked profoundly frightened. The density of bodies in the place, plus the noise, the extremes of shouting, the singing and laughter were a combination powerful enough to overwhelm the senses.

'She's nervous in crowds,' Ethel told William. 'Maybe she should have a short to pull her together.'

William got Aggie a glass of port and ordered halves of bitter for himself and Ethel. 'Don't want to get too far gone,' he said, winking.

Ethel was still wondering about his 'business' with the doctor. She was aware he had something important to tell her, and she was anxious to know what it was. Even so, she could see that William wanted to do things at his own pace, so she didn't press him. Instead, she linked her arm in his and kissed his cheek.

'Happy VE Day, William.'

'Same to you, love.'

A young man suddenly appeared beside them, popping out of the surrounding crush. He grinned at William.

'Blimey, Kevin, you look like you've been through a thresher.'

'I feel like it.' Without waiting to be introduced, the newcomer told the girls he was Kevin Hooper, a workmate of William's. He had a confident, tight-moulded face with wide brown eyes that looked permanently prepared for surprise.

'I've heard a lot about you, Ethel.' He turned to Aggie and pursed his lips for a moment. She was looking less perplexed now. She managed to smile at him. 'I haven't heard a thing about you,' he said.

Over the next few minutes Ethel became intrigued with Kevin's style. She scarcely heard what William was saying, or noticed what was going on around her. With supreme self-assurance, the young man had established a conversation with Aggie, telling her about himself, asking her questions about her work and where she lived, moving by swift stages towards a respectful intimacy; he emanated trust, charm and overwhelming friendliness. By the time it was his turn to order drinks, he had an arm around Aggie. Before the drinks had arrived, she had an arm around him.

'He's doin' all right for himself,' Ethel murmured to William.

'Always does.'

'Bit of a fly man, is he?'

William shook his head. 'Straight as a die. He won't go talkin' her into doin' anythin' she don't want to do. Mind you . . .' He leaned closer. 'He'll have her wantin' to do things she never imagined, before the day's out.'

'I feel a bit responsible for her,' Ethel said, frowning.

'Don't worry. She's in good hands.'

Aggie was under the sway of Kevin's charm. Once or twice she had glanced nervously towards Ethel, but after that she gave every sign of being enthralled.

'Let's take the weight off for a minute.' William pointed to a couple of vacant seats by the door.

As they sat down Ethel was still watching Aggie and Kevin. 'Know somethin'?' she said. 'I reckon this could be her big day. When we came out she was all fidget and fret. She was worried about gettin' too tiddly, bein' in the way an' all the rest of it. Look at her now.'

As Ethel spoke Aggie put her head near to Kevin's and appeared to whisper something. He laughed and drew her towards him with his arm.

'Let's see if we can make it your day an' all,' William said.

Ethel looked at him. His face had turned almost solemn. She didn't believe she had seen him look quite so serious before.

'You know I was talkin' to Dr Legg out there?'
Ethel nodded.

'It was about his house. A bit of his house, that is.'
Ethel anticipated him. 'You're gettin' new digs at last.'
'Well, that's partly it, yes.'

William lived with relatives, and he had told Ethel, several times, how unsatisfactory the arrangement was to him. His lodgings were cheap, but he never felt he could relax in the house. Ethel didn't have to be told any more. Her sympathy was total.

'He's lettin' you have a room, is he? Is it bigger than the one you've got?'

William put up a hand to still her. He wanted to tell it his way. 'A while back I was talkin' to him in here. He told me about this big empty house he's got in the square. He's settin' up his surgery there soon. Wants to do out the rest as flats – an' he'll want a part-time caretaker. It struck me I should get me bid in quick, since . . .' He tailed off, gesturing awkwardly.

'What?'

'Well, you might get mad at me for doin' things back to front, but I thought that maybe it was time . . .' He stopped and looked down at the floor. 'Hell's bells. Now it comes to the bit, I'm gettin' tongue-tied.'

'Tell me,' Ethel urged him.

'You an' me,' he said, looking at her again. 'I reckoned it was time we thought about gettin' married.'

Several things happened to Ethel at once. She let out a gushing, shrill little laugh, the kind she had made in childhood when anybody tickled her. Her mind seemed to spin. It threw forward the memory of what she had said in the taxi; at a deeper level, it cancelled her wistful doubts. A great surge of pleasure rose in her chest, propelling her towards William, making her clasp him tightly.

'Steady, girl. You'll break me ribs.'

'Oh, William . . .'

'Can I take it you think it's a good idea, then?'

She sat back and stared at him. 'Are you tellin' me you've even lined us up with a place to live?'

'It's ours, if we want it.'

She clapped a hand over her mouth. What a day! She stared at William, the source and symbol of all her happiness. Ethel believed she was going to cry.

'Do you want me to ask you properly?'

She nodded, her hand still covering her mouth.

William reached for her other hand. 'Will you marry me, Ethel?'

Her fingers dropped away from her lips. 'Not half, William.'

They hugged each other, oblivious to the noise and revelry surging around them. 'It'll be happy ever after,' William whispered, his mouth close to her ear. 'You wait an' see.'

'I know, I know . . .' Ethel opened her eyes and gazed across the bar, seeing Aggie and Kevin, locked deep in slow-mouthed, intimate talk.

'Who will we tell first?' William murmured.

Ethel moved gently away from him and pointed. 'I think we should let the best man and bridesmaid know as soon as possible,' she said, giggling.

# PART TWO
# After

# 8

Memories of war receded. Then they dimmed. After only a few years they became legend. The unrolling scenario of hardship and deprivation in the 'forties and 'fifties gave way to the self-conscious renaissance of the 'sixties. As that clamorous, swinging decade of permissiveness and hollow culture passed into history, Dr Harold Legg found himself taking frequent stock of his own life and the lives of people with whom he had become intimately, often painfully, involved. In twenty-three years of practice in Albert Square, the doctor had become a vital part of the life in that district; he was guide, confessor and healer to a community that had changed in many dramatic ways, while it stubbornly resisted change at every turn.

On a bright, still-cool July morning in 1970, the doctor paused on the pavement outside his basement surgery. He had done that often lately, almost without thinking. He would stop before going downstairs, like a father taking a fond look at his family before beginning work for the day. He scanned the square and found memories triggered at each turn of his head. It must be his time of life, he thought. Middle age was closing in, comparisons were inevitable and mostly they were sad. It was still the same old square and a lot of the old inhabitants were still there. What saddened him, chiefly, was the memory of loss that accompanied every sign of gain.

He saw Louise Beale cleaning the windows of number 45. If the community had a matriarch, it was her. Lou was tough, indomitable, often coarse and loud, but she was always profoundly humane. She had been a widow for thirteen years. Now her twenty-five-year-old daughter, her husband and their two children lived with her. The younger of the children, Michelle, was only weeks old and had given Louise as many sleepless nights as she had caused her parents. At a time when she should be slowing down, Louise Beale led as busy and harassed a life as she had twenty years ago. Dr Legg made a mental note to quiz her about her rheumatism. Silent suffering was a vice with women like Louise.

By the Bridge Street side of *The Queen Victoria* Louise's son, Pete, was setting up his fruit and vegetable stall. He had taken over the business from his brother Ronnie a year before and trade was thriving. Against all the odds, Dr Legg reflected, Pete had landed on his feet. At twenty-five – he was Pauline's twin – he was twice-married and had a history of social, financial and domestic upheaval that would have seemed excessive in a much older man. Now, whistling cheerfully as he loaded up the stall, he gave every outward sign of stability and energetic endeavour.

'The resilience of people,' Harold Legg murmured. Turning, he looked up at the front windows of the house. His own resilience was a matter of record. He had set up home here with his young wife during the war, while he was still a student. Two years later, she was killed in their small rear garden when a buried bomb exploded. At that window with its net curtains he had often seen her wave to him as he went off to the hospital. She would have been forty-eight by now, the same age as Harold. He sighed and moved to the basement steps.

'Doctor!'

Ethel Skinner had come to the front door. She and William had the ground-floor flat. Scarcely a morning passed when she didn't intercept Harold Legg at some point or other.

'Good morning, Ethel.'

She came down the steps in her apron and slippers. A

mishap with cheap hair dye some years before had left her with a sparse, gingery thatch that she usually kept tucked under a beret, indoors and out. This morning she had introduced a note of variety; her head was turbaned in a bright yellow-and-red scarf.

'I wondered if you might take a look at William some time today.' She stopped on the third step, which kept her head roughly on a level with the doctor's.'

'His chest again, is it?'

She nodded. 'He's wheezin' like a busted squeeze-box. I've told him not to go to work this afternoon. That two-to-ten shift's the hardest one of the lot. He's just not up to it.'

'I'll pop in and see him after surgery,' Harold promised.

'Right, Doctor. Thanks.'

'How about yourself, Ethel?'

'Pardon?'

'How are you keeping?'

'Fit as always, thanks. I've a good constitution, you know that.'

At fifty, Ethel had the speed and stamina she'd had ten years before, but she had grown very thin. She was frankly skinny. Alf Barrett, who had been landlord at *The Queen Victoria* since 1950, had recently run a critical eye over Ethel and announced that he'd seen more meat on a butcher's knife.

'How about the diet sheet I gave you?'

'I've looked at it,' Ethel said evasively.

'I want you to do more than read it. A high-protein diet would put some extra flesh on your bones, Ethel. You need it, with all the running about you do.'

'Yes, well. I've always been slender, I don't think I'm the type to put on much weight.'

'Give the diet a try anyway. Just to please me.'

She smiled coyly, displaying her startlingly white, impossibly regular false teeth. 'I'll get on to it some time this week. I've got other things on me mind, just at the minute.' She held up the fingers of one hand. 'Five days to go. You will come, won't you?'

'I wouldn't miss it for anything.'

Ethel and William's silver wedding anniversary was looming. She had been working on the party plans for over a month. She talked about practically nothing else.

'I'll see you later then, Doctor.'

Harold went downstairs and unlocked the surgery. He took the morning's mail with him to his desk and dropped it on the blotter. The first thing, as always, was to make coffee. He measured the rough, aromatic powder into the percolator jug and switched it on. As he went back to his desk to wait, his mind wandered to the case of William Skinner. He fished the record cards from the file and spread them in front of him.

It was impossible to be thoroughly objective about William as a patient. As a man he was a good friend. Since early in 1947 he had acted as part-time caretaker of the building; during that time he had displayed a calibre of responsibility and concern which went well beyond anything Harold required of him. William regularly cleaned the stairways and the surgery, he made sure that the top-floor tenant obeyed the terms of the lease and paid the rent on time, he made repairs and organized others that were beyond his skill. He was cordial and consistently good-natured. He cherished his wife, provided for her and overlooked her domestic shortcomings. He even let her believe that he couldn't possibly cope without her.

'An upright, downright decent man,' Harold said, examining the records. Also a very sick man, he thought glumly. The clinical history had been established ten years before. The word HAEMOPTYSIS was written in bold letters at the top of a very long, depressing list of successive complaints. The grim-sounding word meant that William had coughed up blood. It was a frightening event for both doctor and patient; Harold remembered William's distress at the time, and his own misgivings. More than two teaspoonsful of bright red blood could mean serious haemorrhage. In William's case the amount he coughed up was much less, but it was still worrying.

After that, there had been only one other occasion when he produced blood. But other symptoms developed rapidly. William was sent to the local hospital for pulmonary function tests. The results were still there in his file, a string of medical hieroglyphics that added up to a picture of a man whose lungs were growing old much faster than the rest of him. Because the condition of the lungs affects the condition of practically every other organ and system in the body, William developed a knock-on chain of degenerative ailments.

Fundamentally, he suffered the combined effects of four long-term afflictions. None of them was curable. In addition, his heart had been weakened by the poor oxygen supply. His general symptoms were shortness of breath, fatigue, bad circulation and occasional, well-concealed depression. The good days were when he could go about his business with only a little discomfort. On bad days William Skinner turned blue and barely had enough breath to speak.

Still thinking about the case, Harold got up and poured himself a cup of coffee. Today, he decided, he would try a new decongestant drug. He had no doubt it was powerful enough to give William relief. But only for a time. Brief respite was all he could offer nowadays, and there was always a price to be paid; next time, it would be harder to do anything to help.

Memory intruded again as he sat down with the coffee. Twenty-five years ago Ethel and William had been one of the liveliest young couples he knew. It was a marriage full of laughter and hope. The years between had flown.

Ethel, always rather odd in her behaviour and dress, had hardened into almost a caricature of the girl she had been; William, once tall, cheerful and robust, now smiled less, stooped and measured his steps carefully, carrying his old charm with a fragile grace.

If nothing else, Harold thought, he could make sure they enjoyed the silver wedding celebrations. He would give William a sufficient jolt of energy to see him past that proud landmark. It was doubtful if he would pass many others.

The wallpaper in the living room had been Ethel's choice. She never tired of the pattern, big splashes of azaleas on a dappled green background, with contrasting posies of buttercups at two-foot intervals. She had been able to find no other paper that pleased her since, so it had seen nine summers on those walls and would no doubt see another four or five before it was finally replaced.

That morning the wallpaper was giving William a headache. But then everything he looked at seemed to make his temples throb. It always struck him as odd that a chest complaint could give him a bad head, but that was the way it went. He sat in his armchair, trying to find something restful to gaze at, picking absently at the shawl Ethel had thrown over his knees.

'Get this down you, William me boy.'

He looked up and saw the big soup mug steaming a few inches from his face. 'Aw, Ethel . . .'

'You've got to keep yourself nourished.'

'But I've had one of them this mornin' already.' Packet soups were something Ethel had taken to with considerable enthusiasm. The ease of preparation was an attraction, certainly, but what she liked most about them was that she could hardly get anything wrong. 'Chicken noodle this one is,' she said, setting the cup on the spindly little table by William's chair. 'Full of goodness.'

'I'm not an invalid, girl.'

'Nobody said you was. But you're poorly, an' poorly people need buildin' up.' She glanced at the book tucked down the side of the chair. 'You been walkin' down memory lane again?'

'I was just lookin', love. You know how I like to. But me head started throbbin' . . .'

Ethel picked up the leatherette-bound picture album. 'Some right old byones in here, eh?' She took it to the little dining table and sat down. 'Dear, dear . . .'

The old pictures always depicted times that seemed forever sunny and happy. Box cameras were faulty tools for recording social history, although that never occurred to Ethel; she never stopped to realize that they were only used when the sun shone, and that nobody ever got photographed without the mandatory cheesy grin.

The pictorial chronology of their life together was laid out haphazardly. The record of summer days often preceded pictures taken that spring; the occasional sparkling wintry scene was followed by pictures taken months before when the leaves were only beginning to fall. In the main they were holiday snaps, taken at Southend, Eastbourne, Brighton and places where they had gone on day outings. Ethel in her one-piece posed identically on beach, balcony and promenade. William, disturbingly, grew old before the browser's eyes. Between 1961 and their last holiday in 1968, he lost much of his hair and weight. Deep lines appeared on his cheeks and around his mouth. The vigour disappeared from his stance.

'Oh, look . . .'

William knew what picture it was, without straining to see. She always said something like 'Oh goodness', or 'oh, my', or 'Oh, look', whenever she came to it. It was a group snapshot taken by his sister Edie. It showed Ethel, William, Ethel's brother Howard, Aggie and Kevin, posing arm-in-arm outside the Hackney registry office on the day Ethel and William were married.

'A day to remember, an' no mistake.'

William nodded. 'You can say that again.'

It was a day to be recalled with joy and then, inevitably, great pain. Howard had sought out Ethel that very day. With six months still to go before he was demobbed, he had been granted one week's leave to try and locate his elder sister. The younger sister had vanished. With tears the pair embraced, with more tears they marvelled at him showing up on her wedding day. Ethel had cried yet again when Aunt Lily came to the wedding, staying just long enough for the ceremony and to wish them well.

'Lookin' at it, William, you'd think nothin' could go wrong, ever after . . .'

A great deal had gone wrong, however. Howard had been permanently crippled in a transport accident a month later, after surviving the entire war on active service. Aggie and Kevin had married in 1946. By the following year they were separated; Kevin confided to William that he was seeking an annulment because the marriage had remained unconsummated. Aggie told Ethel nothing, indeed she told nobody anything; she became totally uncommunicative and was committed to a mental institution in 1948. She smashed a window and slit her throat on the glass a month before the annulment was due to be granted.

Ethel turned the page sharply, quenching the pain of memory. More readily as the years passed, she was able to shut off hurtful recollection. It was a simple matter of survival, she believed. So much had happened that could accumulate and embitter her to swamp her with grief – if she let it.

'Me at Edie's, in the front garden . . .'

Another happy, smiling picture, Ethel sporting her New Look coat in the fifties. Another dark memory was attached, though; six months after the snap was taken Edie had a stroke and spent three terrible, dumb, drooling, paralyzed years in a chair before death intervened. Ethel flipped towards the back of the album. This was better. Herself and Lou Beale standing outside *The Queen Victoria*; William and Dr Legg outside the house, standing on either side of the post where the doctor's plate was displayed; Lou's daughter, Pauline Fowler, holding her first baby, Mark.

'Show us me favourite,' William said.

Ethel smiled and turned back the leaves. 'There you are.' She got up and put the book on his lap. The picture had been taken in a photographer's studio in 1949. Ethel had had her hair done specially and wore an angora cardigan and a peasant blouse. The photographer had retouched the negative until every natural line had gone from her features, leaving the appearance of wax rather than flesh. But the portrait always made William's heart swell.

'Remember what you wrote on the back?' Ethel asked him.

He removed the picture carefully from the retaining corners and turned it over. The pencil scrawl was still there, an extravagant, poetic act committed under the influence of sentimentality and Guinness: 'My Ethel, The Flower of Albert Square.'

'It's still true,' he said. When he looked at Ethel the old light was in his eyes, an ember now. 'You're still the flower.'

'Old weed, more like,' she said gruffly, colouring nevertheless.

William put back the picture and closed the book. 'I think I'll go out an' stretch me legs,' he said. 'I'm sittin' about here like a pensioner. It'll never do.'

'You'll stay where you are until the doctor's seen you.'

'Oh, Ethel. Have you been botherin' him again? I

told you it's just a bit of chestiness, like I'm always gettin' . . .'

'You'll stay put. An' drink up that soup.'

Ethel went to the kitchen and got her coat from the back of the door. 'I'm goin' over to see that Lou's all right. She looked terrible peaky yesterday. I'll be back before Dr Legg comes.'

William sighed and picked up the soup. He drank a little, waiting for Ethel to leave. When she had gone he got up, went to the kitchen and poured the rest down the sink. While he was there he took a damp cloth and wiped off the splashes she had missed on the top of the cooker.

He went back to the living room and stood by the window. Ethel was at Louise Beale's front door, waiting. She was a whirlwind, he thought, always doing favours, always helping out, eternally concerned about other people.

He wondered how she would manage without him. William didn't exactly believe he was a dying man, but he knew he was ageing fast. He was five years Ethel's senior, but in realistic terms he was much older. She was bound to outlive him, and probably by quite a few years. Sometimes at night, lying awake, he would try to imagine his little Ethel coping on her own. It was a blessing she had friends.

He looked across at the photograph album. It was all there, he thought. The summary of their married history. All that had lain before them that sunny VE Day was past. There were no more horizons, just the happy-sad business of being together at the end of it. William would have liked to challenge the swift passing of their time together. He would dearly love to have most of it again, slowly.

He glanced out at the street and saw an old man leaving the surgery. He looked closer, shocked to see that it wasn't an old man at all. It was Billy Phillips, a man his own age, grizzled and wan-looking. The theft of youth was another matter that niggled William. It was taken from you before you were finished with it. That was bloody unfair.

Impatient suddenly, he decided he would go out for a few minutes' walk, even though it meant Ethel would give him a roasting. He got his jacket and slipped it on, found his muffler and cap and got himself ready. As he reached the door a pain like a hot knife sliced up across his chest. His ears sang and he felt his heart clench for one awful second. Breathless, he turned to go back to the living room. His legs went, suddenly and with no warning. He landed painfully on his knees and had to claw at the wall to stay upright.

'God save us all,' he wheezed. 'Get yourself up, William. This is no way to go on . . .'

On all fours he crawled into the living room, feeling helpless and foolish. With an effort that left him gasping he hauled himself on to his chair. Another couple of minutes passed before he could unbutton his jacket. As he did, the pain tore across his chest again. William dropped back, gasping, willing himself not to panic. It would be all right. It always was, eventually.

At number 45, Ethel stopped in the middle of what she was saying to Louise Beale. She stared at the kitchen wall.

'Et?' Louise peered at her. 'What is it?'

Ethel went on staring for a moment, then looked down, shaking her head sharply.

'Had a bit of a turn, have you?'

'It was nothin'.' Ethel waved her friend's concern aside. It had come to her the way things often did nowadays, without the help of tea leaves or cards or anything else. A sense, a tremor of concern, well pinpointed. It was William. But it was all right. He was fine for now. He wouldn't want her running across to the flat and fussing. He liked her to believe he wasn't that bad at all, really.

'You're sure now?' Louise was already at the cooker, putting the kettle on. 'You've turned a bit grey.'

'It's the change,' Ethel said. She had gone through the menopause nine years before, but she still found it convenient, occasionally, to lay blame in that direction. 'I'll just sit down for a minute.'

'You do that. We'll have us a nice cuppa an' a quiet chat, before young Michelle wakes up an' starts creatin' again.'

Everything was all right, Ethel told herself firmly. She would sit there, have her tea, then go back home and not let on that she knew something had happened.

'Gettin' excited about the big party, are you?' Louise asked. 'It won't be long now, eh?'

'Five days.'

So soon. Twenty-five years, all gone. Ethel's charm-word whispered across her mind. *Infinity*. It was a word that could be interpreted a lot of ways, she realized now. But it still held strong meaning, good meaning. She held on to that notion and told herself to stop fretting, while she was at it. Everything was fine, just fine. For now, anyway.

# 9

The woman was in her late thirties. Louise Beale and her daughter Pauline watched from the front room window as she walked to the garden at the centre of the square and looked around at the houses.

'A bit tarty lookin', isn't she?' Louise murmured.

'Just fashionable, Mum.'

'That wasn't what they called it in my day.' Louise folded her hands across her apron, frowning. 'That skirt's too short for a woman her age. All that make-up, too – I can't understand young girls plasterin' their faces that way . . .'

'Got enough jewellery on her to open a stall,' Pauline remarked. Realizing that sounded a shade catty, she added, 'Her hair's very nice.'

'Peroxide blonde,' Louise sniffed. 'Wonder what she's lookin' for?'

The woman took a piece of paper from her jacket pocket and consulted it. After another look around the square she moved off towards the top end. Louise craned her neck.

'She's goin' to Dr Legg's surgery, by the look of it.'

'Maybe she's a patient.'

Louise had her face close to the glass now, clutching the heavy curtain to keep her balance. 'She's gone up the steps. Must be somethin' to do with that man that lives above Ethel.'

'Could be a friend of Ethel's,' Pauline pointed out. 'Or William's.'

'Don't be daft. They don't know anybody like that.'

The woman clopped smartly up the steps and paused

by the front door. She pressed the bell marked 1B twice, sharply. The door opened and Ethel poked her head around the side.

'Yes?'

'Mrs Ethel Skinner?'

'That's me, yes.' The door opened a little wider. Ethel took in the flashy clothes, the clipped, slightly frizzed hair, the smooth mask of cosmetics. 'Can I help you, at all?'

'I'm Trish.' She smiled tightly. 'Remember?'

Ethel put a hand to her cheek. 'Trish? *Our* Trish?'

'That's right. Are you going to invite me in?'

Her accent was slightly foreign. Northern, maybe. How could this be Trish? Ethel's mind tunnelled swiftly back. She saw a gangly, pimpled thirteen-year-old in a long woolly jumper, baggy skirt and heavy shoes. She couldn't imagine that girl becoming this woman.

'You're looking at me like I'm a ghost, Ethel.'

'Well . . .'

'If it's any consolation, I hardly recognize you, either.'

Ethel stepped back. 'Come in,' she said. She still couldn't find one feature that touched a chord of memory. 'In there,' she said, indicating the living room. 'Excuse the mess.'

William looked up from his newspaper. He offered a tentative smile.

'This is Trish,' Ethel told him without conviction.

'Pleased to meet you,' William said, questioning Ethel with his eyes.

'I wondered if maybe you'd remember this.' The woman held out a small crocheted purse. 'I've hung on to it all these years.'

'Oh, yes . . .' Ethel took it, turning it in her hands. 'Nineteen thirty-nine I made that. One for Trish, one for Mum . . .' She fingered the embroidered letter P, for Patricia. When she looked up there were bright, sudden tears in her eyes. 'It's been . . .' She stopped herself and pointed to a chair. 'I'm sorry. Sit down.' Flustered, she dabbed her eyes and drew the chair back from the table. 'It's such a shock.'

William began to understand. 'Ethel's young sister Trish, are you?'

'That's right.' She sat down and put her handbag on the table. 'It's been a long time . . .'

'Twenty-eight years, near enough,' Ethel said.

William pushed himself slowly to his feet. 'You sit down, Ethel. I think we all need a cup of tea.'

Trish's story emerged piecemeal over the next fifteen minutes. When she was evacuated to Yorkshire, she explained, she was placed with a farmer's family who didn't like her, or the other two children billeted with them. Before she was fourteen she had run away, leaving all her identification papers behind. Picked up by the police, she lied about her age and background. In time, after a year in an orphans' centre near Barnsley, she ran away again, lied about her age once more and found work in a munitions factory.

'I met Robbie there,' she said, lighting one cigarette off the stub of another. 'We got married in 1944 and moved out to Skipton. He was a time-served plumber. He opened his own business and we did quite well.'

'What happened after that?' Ethel hadn't taken her eyes off her sister since she began talking.

'Oh, we drifted apart. There was someone else . . .'

'You went away with another man?'

'Well.' Trish laughed nervously. 'That's putting it a bit bluntly, Ethel, but yes, I took up with a chap from York. A salesman. He was in textiles . . .'

'How old was you then?'

Trish frowned. 'I'm not sure. I'd be about twenty, twenty-one. Something like that. Anyway, we got married

97

finally and moved to Bradford, which was nearer to his head office.'

Ethel had drained her teacup. She glanced down at the leaves. A black cloud was what she saw, or chose to see. 'Didn't you ever want to get back to London? Back to Mum and Dad?'

There was a momentary hard glint in Trish's eyes. She composed her hands on the table, the smoke pluming sensuously over her knuckles. 'Frankly, no. The day they sent me away I felt they'd chucked me out. I was sure they didn't want me.'

Ethel remembered the tears, the pleading. Trish hadn't wanted to go, that was for sure. But her mother was frightened for her, she would have liked them all to leave London at that time.

'There wasn't a day passed that Dad didn't talk about you. He missed you bad, Trish. Mum never said as much, but she cried a fair bit.'

Trish shrugged. 'See it from my side. I was a kid, never been far beyond Camden Town in my life, then suddenly I'm told I've got to go and stay in Yorkshire. It was a world away. I never felt so rejected in my life. Once I'd got away from that farm I swore I'd make my own way in life.'

'What brings you back to London, after all this time?' William asked her.

'I've been here for a year now.'

'With your husband?' Ethel asked quickly.

'No.' Trish flicked her cigarette at the metal ashtray William had put on the table. 'We're separated. I came here to take up a job with the London office of a Yorkshire insurance company. It took me a while to find out about the family – the bombing at Beryl Avenue, and so on. Nobody could tell me about you or Howard.'

'He lives in Southend. Got crippled at the end of the war . . .'

98

'I know. Once you get to understand the network of records kept by insurance companies, you can find out a lot. That's how I finally traced you, Ethel.'

By the late 'fifties Ethel had almost stopped wondering about her sister. She had heard countless stories of evacuated children going their own way and never returning home. She had held a faint hope that Trish might turn up one day. Now that she had, Ethel was beginning to feel something like a sense of loss.

'Where do you live?' William asked.

'Fulham. We rent an apartment on Rostrevor Road – me and the chap I live with, that is. It's turning quite fashionable, that area,' she added.

With her history up to date, Trish appeared to have no more to communicate. William coughed to fill the abrupt silence. Ethel, for once, didn't seem to have anything to say for herself.

'It's our silver wedding anniversary tomorrow,' William said. 'We're havin' a party over at the Vic on the corner there. You'd be welcome to come.'

'Yes,' Ethel said. 'That'd be nice.'

'Well, actually . . .' Trish shifted uneasily. 'I'll be working tomorrow, unfortunately. I'm on a half-day today, so I thought I'd take the opportunity to come over.' She lit another cigarette, glanced towards the window, then cleared her throat. 'I was wondering if maybe I could have a private word with you, Ethel. It's what I came about – not that I didn't want to see you for yourself, of course.'

William got to his feet. 'Just the excuse I'm after, Trish,' he said, smiling. 'I promised I'd see a chap in the pub for a minute or two this afternoon. To do with the party.' He glanced at Ethel, who obviously didn't want him to go. 'I'll pop across now.'

'Don't you be out long,' Ethel warned him as he put

on his jacket. 'It's his chest,' she explained to Trish. 'He shouldn't be exertin' himself too much, just at present.'

When William had gone Trish became noticeably brisk. She opened her handbag and took out a long sheet of paper with perforations down both sides. 'I dug out this information from the wartime records,' she explained, tapping the paper. 'It's policy details and a record of payments made by our mother and father.'

Ethel saw it coming. She couldn't believe it, but it was happening. After more than a quarter-century of silence, her sister was after her for money.

'What about them?' Ethel asked.

'Well, you'll pardon me for seeming, you know, businesslike about this sort of thing . . .' She smiled tightly. 'It's just that, as I remembered, Mum and Dad always kept a policy for the two of us. Inheritance money, Mum used to call it.'

Ethel nodded, feeling her face tighten.

'Now, as far as I can see, the whole lot went to you.'

'That's right. It did.'

Now Trish's expression changed. She looked at her sister with pained eyes. 'Ethel, it's not something I enjoy bringing up. But lately, I've had to take a good hard look at things. We've got expenses, my chap and me, and he's not been working for a month – he's an entertainer, and there's been some nonsense about contracts. The bills have mounted up . . .'

'An' you decided it was time to find your sister.'

'I remembered there was money set aside. And half of it was rightly mine . . .' She held up the paper. 'It's all here in black and white.'

'I don't doubt it.'

Trish appeared to infer some resistance. 'You appreciate, I'm sure, that if I had to take it further, I could.'

'You don't have to take it anywhere but here. Your eighty-five quid's safe enough.'

Indeed it was. The small legacy had been established a year after Ethel was born. When her sister came along, it had been agreed that the total dividend would be split between them when both parents were no longer alive. It was a loose, undetailed arrangement as insurances went, but it was clear enough. Twenty-three years' weekly payments amounted to a yield of one hundred and seventy pounds and a few shillings at the time of their parents' death. Trish's share had remained in trust for her, in a separate savings account in Ethel's name. On her fortieth birthday Ethel had been told that she could use the money if she wanted to, since the other beneficiary had been untraceable and had made no contact for more than fifteen years.

Trish folded the paper, a little deflated at the absence of any argument. 'Of course,' she said slowly, 'by now it would be quite a bit more, if you'd banked it . . .'

Ethel nodded stiffly. 'There's interest, an' all. Aunt Lily got the cash banked for me back in 1944, the way I asked her to.'

Trish showed a flicker of admiration. 'You never touched it.'

'I nearly did when our Howard got hurt. He needed money bad. He got nothin' off Mum an' Dad, remember. The idea was that the household furniture an' other stuff would go to the lads. But that all disappeared when the doodlebug landed.'

Trish put the paper back in her bag. 'Well,' she said, 'that's that.' She tried for an amicable smile. 'I hate things like this. They can be so sticky. I'm glad we've got it out of the way.'

Ethel stood up. 'I'll get the bank book, sign the slip in the back an' you can get yourself out of the way, too.'

'Oh, Ethel . . .' Trish looked hurt. 'Don't be like that.'

'Like what?' Ethel demanded. 'Annoyed? Bloody angry? It don't do me no good to know me only sister's a

101

heartless leech that looks me up after nearly half a lifetime to get her hands on some money. Money, I might say, that was left her by two good people she turned her back on.'

'You're twisting the facts – '

Ethel's thin cheeks had turned deepest pink. 'I'll twist your neck if you say another word.' She flounced out of the room and was back a minute later with the bank book and a souvenir ballpoint she had picked up in Clacton. She flipped to the transfer slip and signed it with a trembling hand.

'There.' She flung the book down in front of Trish. 'I hope it does you some good.'

Trish stared at her for a moment, then lifted the book and slipped it in her bag. She stood up. 'I'm sorry you couldn't feel a bit more friendly, Ethel . . .'

'An' I'm sorry I couldn't find any cause to.' She strode to the door and pulled it open. As Trish approached her a thought occurred. 'You been to see our Howard, have you?'

Trish avoided her eyes. 'Yes. Last weekend.'

'Got a nice little business, hasn't he? Considerin' he can barely walk, an' started out with nothin'. I reckon he's done all right for himself.'

Trish nodded. 'He's done very well,' she mumbled.

'How much did you get out of him?'

Trish glared at her. 'Very smug, aren't you? I suppose it makes you feel superior, being able to put down the likes of me. You that stayed at home, got everything done for you. Mum even found your jobs for you, didn't she? You got your own roof over your head while I had to get sent away. I had to sleep in a draughty, dirty outhouse and work like an animal. And after that I made my own way, Ethel, I grafted and schemed to stay alive, so don't you dare feel – '

'It don't make me feel smug *nor* superior,' Ethel

interrupted. 'It just makes me feel a bit sick. We all had it tough, one way an' another. You're the only one that was able to turn your back on the rest an' still get a few bob out of them in the end.'

Trish struggled for a retort; with her face still churning she turned suddenly, stamped along the hallway and let herself out.

Later, as she sat waiting for William to come home, Ethel permitted herself a few tears. She had suffered another loss, another cancellation of something wistfully pleasant. The faded memories of her gawky little sister had been wiped out. In their place there was just another painful recollection, to be avoided as best it could. So many bad things had happened, so many good remembrances had been turned dark by later events. It seemed that too many past, important events in Ethel's life could now only hurt her, in retrospect.'

'Right.' she snapped suddenly.

She blew her nose in a wadded tissue and stood up. She had decided. The time for looking back was over. No more memories, no more wounding herself. She'd had a bellyful of that.

'Down with dwellin' in the past, girl.'

It had dawned on her, belatedly, that she reminisced so much because she was afraid of living in the present – and even more nervous about looking forward. But there *was* a present and a future, after all, and they couldn't make her feel any worse than some of those terrible memories. Where was the sense in going through life with eyes fixed permanently over her shoulder?

When William came in he stood looking round the room. 'Trish gone, has she?'

Ethel nodded. 'An' she won't be back.'

'Oh.' He eased off his jacket, watching Ethel, trying to gauge her mood. She was stiffly going about the business of clearing away the teapot, the cups and the dirty ashtray.

'What happened, then?'

'I'll tell you after. Meantime I'm makin' us another pot of tea, then I'm goin' to make sure the caterin' an' the other arrangements have been sorted out for tomorrow. After that, I might make you a special dinner, an' after *that*, I'll let you take me out for a little drink.'

William followed her into the kitchen. 'Ethel. Is everythin' all right?'

She turned to him. 'William, are *you* all right?'

He nodded, patting his chest. 'I feel better than I have for ages.'

'Then everythin's all right.' She dumped the dishes in the sink. 'Tomorrow we're goin' to have the time of our life. You an' me an' our real friends. So. Today everythin's fine, tomorrow everythin'll be smashin'. Could anythin' be better than that?'

'I suppose not.'

'Right. I'll bring you a cuppa in a minute. Go an' sit down an' look forward to it. An' to tomorrow.'

William sighed and went back to the living room. He dropped into his chair and stared at the window. Ethel could be a mystery at times. A really bewildering, perplexing little puzzler. On the other hand, though, she certainly kept life interesting.

# 10

The party had begun stiffly. The formal arrangement of tables in the bar, the stacks of plates flanked by gleaming cutlery and the centrepiece – a blue-and-cream three-tier cake – set a formal tone so unusual in *The Queen Victoria* that people felt they should be on their best behaviour. It was only when Reg Cox accidentally committed an explosive fart during Dr Legg's toast that people began to relax.

William took well to the role of co-celebrity. He circulated about the bar, beaming as he greeted old friends and acquaintances, telling everyone to enjoy themselves. He slapped men's backs as heartily as they patted his, kissed the women with open relish and drank steadily from the engraved tankard the landford had presented to him.

Smart as William looked in his best suit, new shirt and tie, he was easily overshadowed by Ethel. She had decided to wear a low-cut, floor-length, salmon-pink dress with a black lace overlay. Her hair was a froth of curls, painstakingly created that afternoon by a local hairdresser. Her accessories included a jangling charm bracelet, a diamante necklace and pearl-drop earrings. On her wrist she carried a shimmering evening bag which almost matched her mustard linen gloves.

'You look a fair treat,' Louise Beale told her. 'A proper little duchess.'

'I feel more like a queen, the way I'm bein' treated,' Ethel giggled. 'Aren't people nice? I think I've had a kiss off every man here.'

'If you've had one off Reg Cox,' Louise grunted, 'I should watch you haven't caught somethin'.'

Ethel looked along the bar to where Reg was slurping ale through a mouthful of cake. 'He's a pig, isn't he? I had to invite him, though, much as I can't stand him. He's been in the square all these years . . .'

Most locals assumed that Reg didn't have a friend in the world – he certainly had none in Albert Square. A lifelong bachelor, he had a long history of scrounging, petty thieving and all-round malevolence. He was built to match his record; stooped, tousled and grubby, he glared at the world through oily, pink-rimmed eyes. As Ethel and Louise watched him he swallowed the wad he had been chewing, then snatched another angel cake and crammed it into his mouth.

The landlord, Alf, leaned across the bar. 'Good old Reg,' he said, grinning. 'He's all armpit, isn't he? He's had twice as many cakes an' sandwiches as anybody else, an' he nicked that drink he's got.'

Ethel smiled. 'Tonight, Alf, I'll forgive anybody anythin'.'

'Enjoyin' it, are you?'

'It's all I wanted it to be.' She put an arm round Louise. 'Me, me old man an' all our friends, whoopin' it up on the big anniversary. It's magic, Alf.'

For Angie Watts the party was rather less than magic. She was leaning on the wall by the jukebox, listening to her husband trading banter with his oldest mate, Pete Beale. The couple hadn't been invited officially, but Ethel had seen them stick their heads into the room and had insisted they join in. They accepted, since they had nothing better to do. Den and Angie had been married for only a short time, but already there were signs of disenchantment. Angie groaned softly as Den launched on another wave of reminiscence.

'How about that time you got caught with two pocket-fuls of plastic dart flights? You told the copper they were spares you always carried on you – but you'd gone an' lost your arrows somewhere.'

Pete laughed. 'Remember when you was – what, ten? Eleven? You lifted a watch strap down at Woolies an' hid it in your mouth.'

'That'd be no bother,' Angie drawled. 'There's room enough in there to turn a bus.'

Den scowled at her. As he saw it, his wife just hung about with him so she could get plenty of sniping practice. On top of that, she had too much of a roving eye for a married woman.

'Why don't you go an' waggle your arse at a pensioner, Ange?'

'Shut it.'

Den's face went mock-concerned. 'Not feelin' well, love? Sickenin' for somethin', are you? I mean, you've been here twenty minutes an' you haven't even touched anybody up yet.'

Angie clamped her mouth tight and stared at the list of records on the jukebox. From her point of view, Den took her out with him for decorative purposes; he seemed to enjoy his mates' company a lot more than hers. But in spite of the problems and the perpetual bitching, Den and Angie were united by their ambition to get on, which made up for a lot. Angie believed they had the air of winners about them. And, as she kept reminding herself, they made a great-looking couple.

'How are you gettin' on with your mum these days?' Den asked Pete. 'Things still a bit stormy?'

'Only when I get anywhere near her,' Pete said. 'Everythin's goin' fine, I keep tryin' to tell her that, but she won't have it.' Pete had re-married a year before. His mother regarded his new wife, Kathy, as a home-breaking scrubber who would wreck his life, sooner or later. 'An' there's a baby on the way,' he sighed. 'I wish to God I could straighten things with the old lady before it arrives.

Still.' He shrugged. 'We've all got problems, eh? What about you two? You plannin' a family?'

Angie rolled her eyes.

'She's worried about spoilin' her figure,' Den said.

'It's not that at all, Pete,' Angie hissed. 'It's just that sex makes me ill. Well, the way he does it, anyway.'

Before any real bickering could break out there was a loud accordion fanfare from the other end of the room. William stepped forward, red-faced, coughing into a furled hand as he prepared to make an announcement.

'Ladies and gentlemen . . .'

'Who started lettin' *them* in here?' somebody yelled.

William put up a hand for silence. 'I won't keep you a minute,' he said. 'All I want to do is thank each an' every one of you for comin' here tonight an' makin' this such a great evenin' for the wife an' myself. We've not had a celebration like it ever, an' we're never likely to again.'

As a few people applauded, William extended a hand towards Ethel. She stepped forward with a purse-lipped smile. 'To Ethel, I want to say another public thank-you. For twenty-five years – an' it can't have been easy for her, puttin' up with me every day – she's made my life a garden of delights, with herself the crownin' glory, the loveliest flower of all.'

As everyone cheered and the accordionist struck up with *The Anniversary Waltz*, Ethel threw her arms around William and pressed her face to his shirt. Smiling down at the top of her head, William began moving slowly, guiding her into the gentle steps of the dance.

Louise Beale turned away and buried her face in her handkerchief. Arthur Fowler tapped his wife Pauline on the shoulder and led her into the small dancing space between the tables. Three or four other couples began dancing, too.

'Lord.' Louise blew her nose loudly. 'It's like in the pictures.'

The sentimental atmosphere lasted only as long as the tune. As Pete Beale came to the bar to order a round of drinks his mother turned on him. Her eyes, still red from her small bout of weeping, fixed on his with the intensity of judge's.

'Out on your own?' she demanded.

'That's right, Mum. Kathy's a bit tired . . .'

'Up to your old tricks already. Leavin' the wife at home an' goin' out sniffin' round like a street mongrel . . .'

'Aw, leave it out, will you? I come here because Ethel an' William invited us.'

'If your missus couldn't come, neither should you.'

Pete stared at her. 'You what? Suddenly she's the missus, is she? Last I heard, the Happy Hooker didn't have a look in. Accordin' to you, Kath was all that was rotten, an' then some.'

'It's not the point,' Louise said haughtily. 'If you've got an arrangement, you honour it.'

'So what's so dishonourable about me havin' a drink an' a laugh with a few friends?'

'Your wife's sittin' at home pregnant.'

'Didn't our Dad ever leave you on your own for an hour or two when you was expectin'?'

'That was different,' Louise snapped. 'We're not talkin' here about Albert Beale, God rest his soul. We're talkin' about his tearaway son.'

As Pete and his mother continued to bark at each other, Den and Angie withdrew to a corner seat. Den was looking around the pub as if he were seeing it for the first time.

'What're you lookin' at?' Angie asked.

'This. The place. It's great, isn't it?'

'It's a pub.'

Den sighed. 'There's pubs an' pubs. I reckon I could

make a go of this one. Turn it into the best place in Walford.'

'Walford,' Angie said glumly. 'Big deal.'

'Why not Walford?' He looked around again. 'There'd need to be a few changes, of course . . .'

'You'd need a change on your birth certificate, for a start. You're not twenty-one yet.'

He glared at her. 'You're always makin' difficulties, aren't you? If I get me plans laid now, before I'm thirty I could have the tenancy of a place like this. Matter of fact, this is the one I'd like.'

Angie was nodding, wearing what he called her acid mouth. 'Be lovely, wouldn't it? Back here among your mates, mixin' with all the old riff-raff. That'd really be gettin' on in life, wouldn't it?

'There's worse places we could be, Angie.'

'That's true. At least round here you could play the big fish in the little pond.'

'Aw, bollocks.'

Pete came over with the drinks. 'Right ol' bull an' cow I've just had,' he muttered, setting down the glasses. 'I can't say nor do nothin' right, far as Mum's concerned.'

'I know the feelin',' Den grunted.

Louise was drumming her fingers on the bar top when Ethel came across. 'You don't look like you're enjoyin' yourself, Lou.'

'Yes I am, Et. It's just that I've been havin' words with young Pete. I'll be all right in a minute.'

Ethel fanned herself with her evening bag. 'I'm havin' a great time. I've spent weeks tryin' to imagine what it would be like, what might go wrong. But nothin's gone wrong an' it's turned out a lot better than I ever thought an' it's – ' She stopped suddenly, staring at the door.

Louise looked. A rather handsome man in his fifties

was standing there. He ran his eyes around the crowded bar. When he saw Ethel he appeared to stiffen.

'It's Kevin.'

'Who?'

'Kevin Hooper. He was one of our witnesses when we got married.'

'The one whose wife . . .'

Ethel nodded.

He came across, his arm outstretched. 'Hello, Ethel.'

'Kevin.' Ethel squeezed his hand. Another face from the old days, she thought. Banishing the past was hard to do when memories came at you in the flesh.

'Eleven years,' Kevin said. 'You've hardly changed.'

'Nor you.'

Neither one had told the truth, but kindness was the only impulse; kindness and truth, in this instance, had little in common.

'How did you know about tonight?' Ethel asked.

'William wrote to me.'

'Goodness. He never told me.'

'He wanted to surprise you, he said. I wasn't sure I would come, not until a couple of hours ago. Then I decided I couldn't miss an occasion like this.'

Ethel introduced Louise. For a few minutes the three exchanged pleasantries, then Louise diplomatically excused herself. She could tell there was a lot Ethel wanted to know, but wouldn't ask while she was there.

'Tell me what's been happenin' to you all this time,' Ethel said as soon as Louise had gone. 'How did William find you?'

'He wrote to my old address. I only live a couple of streets away from there. The people passed the letter on.'

The vivid brown eyes still had that quality of readiness, Ethel noticed, as if he were expecting a startling piece of news at any moment. But the rest of the his

111

face was older, slacker. Close up, Kevin had a look of defeat.

'Not a lot's happened to me,' he went on. 'I'm still single. Still doin' the same as before, except I'm in a different dock now.'

He had never tried to stay in touch. Ethel supposed it had something to do with what happened to Aggie.

'You should have come an' seen us before now.'

'Yeah. I suppose I should.' He looked round him for a moment. 'Brings back memories, this place.'

It was where he met Aggie, Ethel recalled. Poor Aggie. Keen as Ethel was to leave the old wounds alone, she also knew that particular one had to be cleansed before it would stop throbbing. She would need to know more before she could leave Aggie firmly in the past. The girl's death, the mystery of it, the sheer unlikeliness of the whole story was an aggravation that had never stopped troubling Ethel. Looking at Kevin now, she knew she would get him to talk about it, sooner or later.

'So where's William?' he asked.

'Takin' a walk round the square, love.' She tapped her chest. 'He's got to get out in the air if he's in a stuffy place more than an hour or so. He's all right. Dr Legg's gone with him.'

At that moment William was leaning on the railings by the central garden, slowly breathing the night air. Beside him Dr Legg stood humming softly, listening to the distant sounds of traffic.

'What's the full score, Doctor?'

In the shadowy lamplight Harold could see William's face only faintly. There was no mistaking the intensity in his eyes, though.

'About your health?'

'I suppose tonight's not the time to ask, or to be thinkin' about these things,' William sighed. 'But I *am*

112

askin'. Back then, just before we came out, I come over very strange. Not the pains this time. More a weakness, in every bit of me, like all me blood had been taken away.'

'It was the excitement.'

'The excitement on top of what?'

Harold didn't reply for a moment. 'On top of a fairly serious illness,' he said at last. 'The full score, as you put it, is that you'll soon have to give up work altogether. When I can be sure you're not overdoing things, I'll be able to control your condition better.'

'Sometimes I think I've not got long to go.'

Harold patted his shoulder. 'We all think that, once we're past a certain age. Hardly a week passes when I don't imagine I've got the beginning of something that'll see me off.'

'I worry a lot about Ethel.'

'You shouldn't. She's a very capable lady.'

William laughed softly. 'In her way. She's that scatterbrained, I wonder how she'll get on without me holdin' her reins.'

'You were right, a minute ago,' Harold said.

'How do you mean?'

'When you said tonight's not the time to be thinking about these things. This is a great occasion in your life, William. You should be back in there enjoying it.'

'I suppose you're right.'

'Come on, then.'

They sauntered across to the pub. 'Just remember,' Harold said, holding open the door, 'Walford cemetery's full of people who probably wish they'd spent less of their time worrying, and more of it enjoying their lives.'

As soon as William walked into the pub he saw Kevin. Their reunion was warm and emotional. With his arm around Kevin's shoulder William introduced

113

him to the doctor, then to a half dozen other people at the bar.

Ethel appeared with a glass in each hand.

'Isn't it lovely to see him again, William?' She was flushed, her eyes bright with pleasure and drink. She held up the glasses. 'Look at these. Everybody's bein' so generous.

'You could always say no,' William pointed out.

'I never learned how, when it came to shorts.'

Kevin laughed. 'Are most of these people your friends?'

'I'll say.'

'They all seem to be in lively spirits.'

'Listen,' Ethel said. 'Lou an' her son Pete have just had a barney, the two lads off the rug stall are arguin' over a girl, Den and Angie Watts are havin' their own ding-dong in the corner, an' the guv'nor's given Reg Cox a right earful for pocketin' a half bottle off the bar.' She giggled, spilling drink on her fingers. 'Nobody's on their best behaviour. Isn't that marvellous?'

# 11

A few minutes after midnight, alone by the fireside in the flat, Ethel and Kevin sat drinking the remains of the red wine he had brought. The party had finished just after eleven and Kevin had been persuaded to come back for a late drink. At a quarter to twelve, after extracting a promise that Kevin would visit them again soon, William had gone to bed bone-weary, hardly able to keep his eyes open.

The talk, under Ethel's guidance, had finally got around to Aggie. Kevin spoke about her haltingly, the emotion swelling his throat. He spoke of how he missed her, how he had gone on loving her even though he had walked out of their home.

'Not a day passes but I think about her, Ethel.'

'I never understood. None of what happened sounded like her. Not Aggie.'

Kevin looked at her gravely. 'I've thought, all these years, that you might be blamin' me.'

'Never once,' Ethel assured him. 'I never knew enough to lay any blame.'

'I was sure of it, to tell you the truth. I've wanted to get in touch with you an' William a lot of times, but I always stopped myself, thinkin' how hard it would be to face the accusation – whether you came out with it or not.'

'Kevin, tell me. Did you – well, did you understand what it was that went wrong? It's nagged me a lot, wonderin' . . .'

He nodded. 'It took a bit of time to get it straight in me mind. But yes, I understand. Aggie wanted to settle down with a family. She wanted that real bad. She had to be like other women.'

'I remember her sayin' as much. It all sounded normal enough to me.'

'She wanted to have it all around her. But she didn't want to go through the moves, Ethel. It was a kind of status for her. She wanted it given. She wasn't up to buildin' it.' He smiled shyly, showing no trace of his old self-assurance. 'I fell in love with her, you know. For real, an' that was somethin' I'd never done before.'

'William told me at the time. You was head over heels, he said.'

'But when you two thought that me an' Aggie were, you know, gettin' up to things . . .' He cleared his throat nervously. 'There was nothin', Ethel. There wasn't even much happenin' in the kissin' an' cuddlin' department.'

That came as a big surprise to Ethel. She had been under the impression – largely given by Kevin, it was true – that they were lovers long before they were married.

'She tried, of course. But there was somethin' lackin' in the girl. She hated the intimate side of marriage. I've been told, since, that a lot of women an' men are like that. It wasn't somethin' I could understand at the time, though. I'd thought once we were wed, everythin' would be OK.'

'But it wasn't.'

'No, it got worse. She used to clench her teeth when I touched her. An' she went quiet, terrible quiet. Days an' days of silence, sometimes.'

'The poor love,' Ethel murmured.

'Poor me, that's what I kept thinkin'.' Kevin said. 'I gave it up in the end, you know all about that. She didn't want me to go. She even begged me to stay. I was her idea of a perfect husband, see? I was one of the things she needed round her. But I couldn't take it – I just

116

about went off the rails with the frustration, the strain, not bein' able to share even her moods with her . . .'

'An' did nobody know what made her that way?'

'Not really. But the thing about her mother – that seemed to make it worse.'

'Her mother?' Ethel had met her once, a sullen, withdrawn old woman – too old, it seemed, to be a parent of Aggie's. More like a grannie, she had thought at the time.

'Yes. The old lady died two months after we were married.'

'Oh dear . . .'

'Aggie was sure she had killed her. Her mother didn't like me, you see. She'd told Aggie she didn't want her marryin' me. But Aggie wanted that status, to be a married woman . . .' Kevin shook his head. 'It was all a very bad mess, Ethel. At the end, Aggie was what they call a manic depressive. They tried to explain it to me, at the hospital. Most of what they told me went over my head. But it had a lot to do with her mind an' her body bein' strangers to each other.'

'God Kevin, I'd never have guessed.'

For over a minute they sat in silence, Ethel sipping her wine, Kevin looking at the fire.

'The upshot's no more than I deserve, I suppose,' he said finally.

'What do you mean?'

'The way I am. I can't even speak to another woman now. Not in the old way. I've been livin' like a monk, practically from the day an' hour I met Aggie.'

Ethel didn't understand. She was sure it wasn't the wine. Her head seemed clear enough. 'Why couldn't you put her death behind you, Kevin? It's a long time ago, an' it's not as if any of it was your fault . . .'

'But it was. If you *had* blamed me, you'd have been

right. The guilt of it still brings me to tears at times. If I'd not left her – '

'She would have done it anyway.'

Kevin stared at Ethel. 'How can you know that?'

'How can you know any different? Kevin, have you ever talked to anybody else about it – all this you've told me?'

'No. I don't know many people that well.'

Ethel nodded firmly. 'Exactly. So you've bottled it all up an' got it twisted so bad you think you were to blame. I'm no doctor, God knows, but I know this.' She leaned forward. 'Now listen to me. If you'd stayed you'd have made her just as bad as she turned out in the end. All them silences, an' her not wantin' to be touched, that would have set in real hard an' you'd both have wound up bein' mental cases.'

'But . . .'

'I know a thing or two about people with trouble in their minds, Kevin. I was one of them myself. I went a bit mental when I lost my parents an' everythin' I owned. I wasn't too bad, as it happens, but I was bad enough, an' I saw plenty that makes me understand some of them cases can't be helped. I don't think you've anythin' to blame yourself for.'

'Do you really think that? Or are you tryin' to make me feel better?'

'Both. I believe it, an' I want you to buck up.'

Kevin went silent again. Ethel was sure she knew what was happening. He had spoken to someone for the first time – to a woman, too, which had to make a difference. For once he had been given an answer that wasn't of his own making.

He finally put down his glass and stood up. 'Ethel. I want to thank you for listenin' to me, an' for what you've said. You've helped me . . .' He still looked troubled. 'I'm not sayin' you've convinced me . . .'

'Give it a chance, Kevin. Feelin' guilty's no use, anyway. We're all poor things, strugglin' for the best. An' remember – there's no sense ruinin' your own life frettin' about one that's finished.'

When he had gone, after thanking her again, Ethel decided to sit down with the half glass that remained of the bottle.

'What a time I've had,' she cooed at the dying coals.

The silver wedding celebration couldn't have gone better. She hadn't enjoyed herself so much for years. The same went for William. They had both felt that thrill again, the long-lost sense of being luck's children. As if that hadn't been enough, she'd had the triple bonus of Kevin showing up. Triple because it had been lovely to see him again, because he'd thrown light on a mystery that had bothered her too long, and because she had managed – she was sure – to steer him away from his haunting guilt.

'Not bad for one day,' she whispered.

Her last thought, before she drained the glass, was of Aggie. Now, at long last, she was properly in the past with all the other sadness.

Ethel stood up and went through to the bedroom. 'RIP, Aggie,' she grunted. Before she had her shoes off, she had begun to wonder what she would make for William's breakfast.

# 12

Towards the end of 1973 newspapers and television bulletins were issuing regular reports about a world economic crisis. It appeared that the root of the trouble was the Arab oil-producing nations, who were restricting supplies of their oil to the rest of the world. There was talk of petrol rationing, power breakdowns, even large-scale industrial collapse. None of it surprised Ethel. She had warned everyone who would listen, months ago, that society as they knew it was practically doomed.

'I don't know about the Arabs', she told Dr Legg in his surgery one afternoon. 'They might have somethin' to do with the world's troubles, but this country's goin' down the pan for reasons of its own.'

'And what would they be?'

Harold Legg looked up from his desk. Ethel had wandered off somewhere with her bucket and mop. Since William had given up work, nearly two years before, Ethel had taken over most of his part-time work, which included cleaning the surgery three times a week.

'Goin' decimal was the start of it.' Her voice preceded her. She appeared in the doorway a moment later, her turban at an unintentionally jaunty angle. 'It threw everythin' sideways. Ten bob had been ten bob since God knows when. Then suddenly it's called fifty pee. An' it's a coin instead of a half-sheet, like it always was, an' ought to have stayed.'

Harold nodded, trying to divide his attention between Ethel and the case record in front of him.

'I mean, what kind of government is it that does away with the half crown? Or the thrupenny bit? Prices have gone crazy because of it. People don't know if they're comin' or goin'.'

'And you believe that's going to ruin the country, do you?'

'Not on its own, no. There's the Common Market. It's madness, us joinin' up with the Germans an' Froggies an' all them other foreigners. We're an island for a good reason, Doctor. We should leave them to get on with their warmongerin' an' eatin' garlic an' all of that.' She shook her head sadly. 'I've never liked the look of that Ted Heath.'

Harold closed the case folder and smiled at her. 'That's it then, is it? We're going over the edge because of decimal coinage and the Common Market?' He wasn't entirely making fun of Ethel. Her philosophy, political views and general moral outlook fascinated him. She was an encyclopaedia of Cockney prejudice. He could, arguably, learn a lot from her.

'The immigrants'll do their share, an' all.'

'The coloured immigrants, you mean?'

Ethel nodded. 'All the really big troubles we've got, they're down to us doin' what isn't natural.' She ticked off the causes of disaster on her fingers. 'Inventin' funny money. Sidin' with people that would cut our throats soon as look at us. Lettin' Pakis, chinkies, blackies an' fuzzy-wuzzies take over our houses an' shops an' factories.' She threw up both hands. 'It's madness. Look at the East End already.'

'It's certainly changed a lot,' Harold admitted.

'Full of foreigners an' their foreign ways. What happened to the pie an' mash shops? The whelk stalls? There's not many fish an' chip shops left, come to that. It's all Indian restaurants nowadays, or Chinese. I don't know how folk get half that muck down them.' Ethel narrowed an eye. 'Have you noticed most of the Jews have disappeared, an' all?'

'I'm still here, Ethel.'

'You know what I mean, though. The old tailors an' dressmakers an' jewellers have vanished.'

'One set of immigrants has moved out, others have moved in.'

'The Jews weren't immigrants though, were they?'

Harold felt the discussion had probably gone as far as it should, for the moment. To take it further, they would have to go into the meaning of the word 'immigrant'. Ethel clearly thought it meant coloured.

He looked at his watch. 'I'll have to get moving. I've some calls to make.' He got up and took his bag from the side table. 'You won't forget to lock up, will you?'

'I won't, Doctor.'

Harold left the surgery and crossed the road to where his car was parked. He got inside, put his case on the passenger seat beside him and sat back for a moment, thinking. Whenever he spoke to Ethel these days, he was conscious of the possibility that, at any moment, she would start asking about William again. This afternoon she hadn't mentioned him once, which Harold counted a blessing. He felt obliged always to steer a middle course between reassuring her and telling her the truth. Reassurances, by now, were thin on the ground.

He looked at his watch again. He would have time to look in at the hospital, he decided. Two days ago William had been taken there for a cardiac and pulmonary check-up. Since the previous December he had been taking powerful stimulant drugs; even with their help, he was seldom fit enough to walk more than a few yards before he became breathless. The question facing Harold was whether he could justify stepping up the treatment. It might improve the quality of William's life, but it would very likely shorten it a little, too. It was an old clinical dilemma; better life, or longer life.

At the hospital he was shown into the office of the

122

Consultant Cardiologist, Dr Webb. They were old acquaintances. Harold worked in the Cardiology Department once a week, and it was because of his connection there that he had managed to have William put through the tests without the usual delay.

'Sit down, Harold.' Dr Webb was short and tubby, a man with a gourmet appetite for food which matched his relish for work. 'How are things out in the jungle of general practice?'

'Same as always, Richard. Hectic.'

They faced each other across the cluttered desk. 'I've come to sound you out on the case of William Skinner. Remember him?'

'Of course.' Dr Webb shifted a pile of papers and drew out a folder from underneath them. 'He was here a couple of days ago. I saw to him personally.'

'That was good of you.'

Webb opened the folder. 'I gave him the works, as you asked.' He picked up a sheet of paper and squinted at it. 'My bloody handwriting . . .' He stared at the sheet in silence for a few moments. 'Well. Do you want the bad news, or the worse news?'

'I might as well have it all.'

'Right. Your patient has a clutch of pulmonary conditions, as you're aware. Until a month or so ago, I'd say, it was a toss-up which would go into a nose-dive first – his lungs or his heart.' He gathered up some other papers and shook them at Harold. 'You won't find a shred of hope in these test results, I'm afraid. His heart is failing.'

'I was afraid of that.'

'I can give you five or six separate causes. There's hypertrophy, severe afterloading, the semilunar valves are out of kilter – it all adds up to congestive heart failure.'

'Left ventricular?'

123

'Yes. And as if that wasn't bad enough, the function tests have thrown up some other nasty little doom-notes as well.'

'Prognosis?'

Webb shrugged. 'If you do your best, which means suppressing the arrhythmias when they occur, increasing his venous tone, stepping up renal blood flow, slowing the heart rate and all the other witchcraft it takes to keep a man in this condition going, I'd say . . .' Again he shrugged. 'Well, with a lot of monitoring, he might have eighteen months or so. Two years at the very most.'

'And that's only if my best is good enough.'

'The engine's worn out, Harold. It could pack in tomorrow, or today. A lot of it depends on the amount of natural fight in the man – or spirit, if you go in for concepts of that kind. We can't go on repairing something that really needs rebuilding. Mr Skinner's in good hands, that's the only encouraging thing that can be said.'

Harold nodded, trying to imagine what he would tell Ethel the next time she asked him.


Later that day, as William was having his customary two hours in bed, Ethel went round to *The Empire*, an old local cinema that had been turned into a bingo hall in the late 'sixties. Four afternoons a week she did part-time cleaning there with Mrs Jarvis, another docker's wife.

Today, for some reason, there was no sign of Mrs Jarvis. Ethel came out of the little store room where they hung their coats and went to the manager's office. Terry Skarrett was sitting on the side of the desk, leafing through the *World's Fair*. He looked up and twitched his thin moustache at Ethel.

'An' what can I do for you, Mrs Skinner?'

'It's Mrs Jarvis. She's not here. She should have been in an hour before me.'

'Ah.' Skarrett stood up, smoothing the back of his

bottle green blazer. 'Mrs Jarvis.' He rubbed his chin, making the dark stubble rasp like sandpaper. 'I had to let her go, I'm afraid.'

Ethel frowned. 'Let her go?'

'I released her from our employ,' Skarrett said. 'Gave her the push. Aimed her.'

'She's got the sack?'

'That's about it, yes.'

Ethel was a little saddened. She liked Mrs Jarvis, principally because she was a good listener. 'What did you get rid of her for?'

'It was a little matter to do with sticky fingers. She was here after the last session yesterday, as usual. When she left the upstairs office she took more than the Hoover with her. To cut a long story short, a spot search of her coat pockets uncovered thirty quid in three plastic bank bags – our bags, Mrs Skinner.'

'Oh, my word.' You just never knew with people, Ethel thought. 'Will this mean I'll have to do the whole auditorium by meself?'

Skarrett shook his head. 'I've got a woman comin' to fill in, just for today an' tomorrow, until I can get a proper replacement for Mrs Jarvis. You'll have to show her the ropes.'

'Fair enough,' Ethel said. 'I'll go an' get a start made.'

She went to the cubbyhole where the cleaning materials were kept. She put on her overall then trundled the big vacuum cleaner out into the passageway. As she began hauling it up the carpeted slope towards the auditorium a woman appeared behind her.

'You Mrs Skinner?'

Ethel turned and saw one of the fattest women she had ever laid eyes on. She was wearing an open tweed coat, revealing a body of dirigible proportions. She stood with spread feet, tilting her head at Ethel. A cigarette end hung from the corner of her mouth.

'I'm Mrs Skinner, yes.'

'I'm Brenda Tully. Mr Skarrett said I should find you.'

'You're the cleaner, are you?'

'Yeah.' Brenda took the dog-end from her mouth and coughed. 'Where do you want me to start?'

As Ethel moved closer to the woman, she realized she must be about her own age. She also observed that Brenda's neck resembled a bundle of quoits.

Ethel pointed to the cubbyhole. 'If you get a brush and pan out of there, you can do the seats an' ashtrays. I'll take the carpets.' She paused. 'I don't think we've got a suitable overall . . .'

'Nobody ever has, love. I've brought me own.'

They made slow progress during the first fifteen minutes. Brenda couldn't get the knack of tipping the ashtrays into her pan. She also found it very easy to get wedged between the rows of seats. Finally Ethel told her to take the Hoover and she'd do the seats and ashtrays herself.

After an hour they took a break. In addition to her own voluminous overall, Brenda had brought along her own tea mug. It was a giant affair that held nearly a pint. As the big woman leaned on the bench in the little kitchen, slurping contentedly, Ethel's curiosity finally became vocal.

'Married are you, Brenda?' Ethel had been trying to imagine how any man could get to grips with a woman that size.

'I'm a widow.'

The reply put a curious pang across Ethel's heart. Widowhood had a relevance to her that she never quite admitted; even so, widows fascinated her. Like a person about to have teeth extracted, she was anxious to have others' views on the experience.

'I'm sorry to hear that,' she said sympathetically. 'Has it been long since your hubby passed away?'

126

'A year.'

A recent widow. More fascinating still.

'It must have been terrible for you.'

Brenda nodded, squashing her neck like a fleshy con-
certina. 'I near went off me head, to tell the truth.' She
took a gulp of tea and fished her cigarettes and lighter
from her overall pocket. 'It was expected, mind you. My
Martin was ill for a long time. Years.'

Ethel was transfixed. 'His heart?'

'No. He'd Parkinson's Disease. Had it a couple of
years before they knew what it was.' She lit up and blew
a derisive plume at the wall. 'Stupid piggin' doctors. I've
never trusted the sods.'

'How did you cope, then? When he'd passed away,
that is?'

'I shut meself in the house for a while. Just couldn't
believe he wasn't *there* – I don't mean not in thc housc,
but not anywhere. He didn't exist. I couldn't get used to
that, it got worse an' worse to think about.'

That would be it exactly, Ethel thought. Not there.
Not anywhere. How could she ever accept that William
wasn't in the world?

'So I went on the drink for about a month. After that it
was eatin'. I ate an' ate an' ate. I've never been small,
but I was nothin' like this size a year ago.'

'But you got over your loss . . .'

'Things got better gradually. My kids were a big help.
I'm fine now.'

So there was nothing to glean from this woman, after
all. Children made all the difference. She remembered
how Louise Beale had drawn strength from the kids when
Albert died. Ethel had never longed for children the way
some women did – which was just as well, since she
couldn't have any. Lately, though, she wished she'd had
at least one child. A son. What a comfort he would have
been.

'What about you, love?'

'Me?'

'You married, or – '

'Married,' Ethel said quickly. 'Twenty-eight years an' a few months.'

'How old's your husband?'

'He's fifty-eight.'

Brenda made a sad little smile. 'My old man was fifty-nine when he died. It's not a long life for anyone, is it, dyin' at that age.'

'No.' Ethel suddenly didn't want to talk about it any more. She looked up at the clock and put on a shocked face. 'God, look at the time. We better get back on the job, or Skarrett'll be after us.'

As the afternoon wore on it appeared that Ethel had opened a floodgate. Brenda kept on about her widowed state, about how different it was from being married, and about all the things she missed. Even the Hoover couldn't drown her out. Ethel hated it. It was one thing to learn about the framework of widowhood; that could strengthen someone's mind and prepare them for the inevitable – even when that someone wasn't prepared to admit to herself what she was up to. Brenda's comprehensive account, right down to the details of sleeping habits, was depressing. The auditorium was large, but by the end of her shift Ethel was feeling shut in.

When Brenda had gone Skarrett came along and asked Ethel how she had performed.

'She's all right. A bit slow maybe, but she's new to the work. An' her size don't help.'

'I was askin' because she put out a sounder about maybe comin' on a regular basis.'

Ethel hoped she wouldn't. Much more of Brenda's chat and she'd go up the pole.

'I really wanted somebody with a decent track record, like your own.' Skarrett looked thoughtful for a moment,

128

then he sniffed dismissively. 'Nah, I don't reckon I want her lumberin' about the place day in an' day out. She'd end up doin' some damage – an' like you say, she's bound to be slow.'

Ethel was relieved.

'See you tomorrow,' Skarrett said, going back to his office.

'Yes. 'Bye, Mr Skarrett.'

As she put on her coat Ethel realized the afternoon's stint had left her feeling drained. She would drop in at the Vic and have a Guinness, she decided, just to keep her strength up.

Going along Bridge Street a few minutes later, she saw Louise Beale entering the pub by the corner door. She had her head down, pre-occupied with something. She didn't see Ethel, who hurried to catch the door before Louise let it go.

Ethel arrived a second late and was almost hit in the face by the door. As she jumped back smartly, she glanced towards the flat. Her heart froze. There was no light in the living room window. William was always up by this time. The first thing he did was put on the light, then make himself a pot of tea. The place was in total, ominous darkness.

For the first time in years Ethel found herself running. She cleared the corner of the square and charged up the steps, gasping and nearly falling as she tripped on the second one from the top.

'God, no, William,' she whimpered, fumbling with her key. She missed the lock three times then located it and wrenched the door open. She dashed into the living room and stood by the table, leaning on it with both hands. The only sound was her own agitated breathing. The place was cold and dark. Lifeless. She dropped her bag on the table and went to the bedroom door. 'Please,

129

please . . .' She closed her eyes for a moment, then pushed the door open.

'Please, God . . .' She crossed to the bed and saw William's pale, motionless head against the pillows. She put out a hand and touched him.

'What?' He rolled on his back suddenly, startling her. 'Ethel?' He rubbed his tongue across his palate, moistening it. 'Glory be, what time is it?'

She couldn't speak.

'I must have needed me sleep.' He pushed himself up in the bed. 'You all right, girl?'

In the darkness she nodded and squeezed his arm. 'Stay where you are,' she managed to say. 'Come round properly. I'll go an' get the kettle on.'

In the kitchen she stood by the sink, her hands trembling so violently she couldn't get the kettle to the tap. Finally she put it back on the cooker and lowered herself on to a chair. She couldn't stop shaking.

'Silly old fool,' she chided herself. William had overslept before, now she thought about it. What was getting into her? She had special feelings about these things, after all. If anything had happened she would have known.

After a minute she stood up again and filled the kettle. That would teach her, she thought. In future she would steer well clear of women who talked about their late lamented spouses. It just wasn't healthy to listen to that kind of talk. And it wasn't healthy to encourage it in the first place, a small voice told her.

# 13

In 1975 two notable changes occurred in the square. A Bengali family called Jeffrey bought a small self-contained flat adjacent to *The Queen Victoria* and opened a general food store on Bridge Street, next door to the launderette. A short time later Alf Barrett and his wife Polly retired from the pub; to the surprise of many locals the new tenant turned out to be Den Watts. At a pre-takeover party Den promised that when he took charge, the Vic would continue to maintain the solid traditions of quality and service for which it had always been well-known. He added that he planned a number of improvements, though he didn't say what they would be.

On Den's first day as tenant, Pauline Fowler and her husband, Arthur, stood by their gate and watched as he put up the new licensee's board. Pauline nudged Arthur. 'What kind of a guv'nor do you think he'll make?'

'It's hard to say. He's keen enough, but twenty-five's kind of young to be takin' on a place like that.'

'Yeah, that's what Mum said. She's a bit suspicious about the so-called improvements he's goin' to make, an' all. I mean, what can he do to improve the Vic?'

'Maybe Angie's goin' to open a knockin' shop at the back.'

'That's not very fair, Arthur. Angie's a bit flighty, that's all. I reckon she'll make a good landlady over there.'

'She's brassy enough for the part.'

Pauline watched Den drive in the last screw, concentrating as if she were doing it herself. 'I don't think it's any life for a kiddie, though. I went to school with a girl that grew up in a pub. She said they'd no real home life.'

'Well,' Arthur sighed, 'that's a hazard of the job. When all the punters are windin' down, the guv'nor an' his missus have got to get wound up. They're in show business, aren't they? Like you say, it's no life for a young kid, but there's bound to be casualties in that trade.'

Ethel had wandered across the square and was standing beside Pauline. 'That poor little lamb of theirs has had a bad enough start as it is,' she said.

'What do you mean?' Pauline asked her.

'Adopted, isn't she? She's bound to know in her heart that Angie's not her real mum.'

Arthur frowned. 'How do you make that out?'

'Stands to reason. The young, whether they're fish, flesh or fowl, always know their own mothers.'

'But not their fathers, eh?'

'It's a wise child that knows that, Arthur.' Ethel chuckled. 'Anyway, I'll make sure little Sharon gets plenty of pamperin', just to make up for what she's missin' in other directions.'

Pauline asked her, jokingly, if she were moving into the pub as a baby minder.

'No, nothin' like that. I'm goin' to help out with the cleanin'. Den asked me yesterday. Not a bad job, Pauline, an' it's nice an' handy.'

'Polly Barrett always did her own cleanin'.'

'Angie's got her nails to think about,' Arthur pointed out.

The matter of Ethel's cleaning job was raised a couple of minutes later as Den went back into the pub, carrying the folding steps. Angie was standing behind the bar in a tight, orange polo-neck sweater, her tightest black skirt and glossy black break-neck high heels.

'I've been thinkin',' she said.

'Don't go strainin' anythin', now,' Den warned, leaning the steps against the bar.

'Listen, I'm bein' serious. I don't think I want that Ethel Skinner doin' our cleanin'.'

Den smiled tightly. 'Don't you? Well I do, Ange. An' it's all arranged.' He rolled down his shirt sleeves. 'Was there anythin' else?'

'It's a bad move. She's a nosey, gossipin' old cow. Nobody can hiccup round here without her knowin' about it. I don't want her stickin' her hooter in our business.'

Den rubbed his hands together slowly. 'I agree with you,' he said. 'Ethel does gossip, an' she's pretty nosey. But so are all the other old dears round here. The difference with Ethel is she's got experience for the job, an' she's dead honest.'

'There's bound to be somebody else you could get.'

'Yeah, I'm sure there is. Some biddy that'll give the place a spit an' a lick an' rob us blind.'

Angie folded her arms stubbornly. 'There's honest an' honest, Den. For all we know, Ethel could come in here every mornin', make her first stop at our broom cupboard an' the second one at the rum optic. She likes her drink, an' there's some people don't think it's robbery to take the odd nip.'

'She wouldn't do that,' Den said. 'Apart from anythin' else, she couldn't reach the rum optic.'

Angie sighed. 'I just don't like it. The thought of her livin' practically on the doorstep, an' spendin' a couple of hours every day roamin' about our private quarters . . .'

'She'll only be doin' the bars.'

'There's nothin' to stop her goin' upstairs if she feels like it. She's built like a bloody ferret, we wouldn't even notice.'

'The matter is closed,' Den said firmly. 'Ethel's been told the job's hers. If she doesn't come up to scratch, we'll sack her later on.' He glanced at his watch. 'Bloody hell. Ten minutes to openin'. I'll nip downstairs to check everythin's all right in the cellar, then we'll be off.' He leaned across the bar and kissed Angie's forehead. 'Cheer up. This is it. The big day. First impressions are important with the crowd round here.'

Angie smiled, reluctantly. 'I won't let you down.'

'I know you won't. Just switch on the smile, stick out the boobs an' you can't go wrong.'

As Den went off to the cellar the corner door opened and Ethel stepped inside.

'We ain't open yet,' Angie said icily.

'I haven't come as a customer, love. Well, I'll be a customer as soon as you're servin', but what I mean is, this is business.'

Angie shifted her weight from one hip to the other. 'You'll have to wait till Den's finished in the cellar.'

Ethel came to the bar and rested her elbows. 'You'll do just as well, Angie. It's about me hours – on the cleanin', like.'

'I told you, you'll have to – '

'Y'see, what with William bein' as bad as he is, I have to keep lookin' in on him. Sometimes he can't turn himself in the chair, because of the congestion. What I was wonderin' was, if I nipped back to the flat say every twenty minutes – '

'Den!' Angie yelled.

He appeared from the cellar door with a spanner in his hand. He nodded to Ethel and raised his eyebrows at Angie.

'Your cleaner wants to talk her timetable.' Angie turned and flounced off through to the back.

'What's the trouble, Ethel?'

She explained again. 'Of course,' she added, 'I'd work the full amount of time I'm supposed to. I wouldn't be cheatin' you out of the odd five minutes I take off.'

Den nodded amiably. 'I'd see you didn't anyway.'

'It's all right with you then, is it?'

'Of course it is.' Den looked at the clock. 'We're not officially open yet, but how do you fancy bein' me first customer?'

'Oh.' Ethel stood back from the bar, looking around as if she would have liked an audience to observe this honour Den was bestowing on her. 'Don't mind if I do. I'll have a Guinness, please.'

'Comin' up.' Den picked up a bottle and prised off the cap. As he poured the rich dark liquid into a glass he said, 'This is on the house, Ethel. An' while you're here, maybe you could do me a favour.'

'Of course, love.' Ethel reached out and took the drink from him. 'Here's health, wealth an' everythin' you wish yourself.'

'You just wished me everythin' I wish meself, ta very much.'

Ethel took three swift swallows from the glass and set it down. She wiped her mouth with the back of her hand and beamed at Den. 'Now then. What's this favour you want doin'?'

'It's Sharon,' he said. 'Round about now she gets restless. Up till today, she's been taken out for a walk about this time every mornin'.'

Ethel nodded. 'No trouble, Den. I like walkin' with kiddies. They're good company.'

'No, I don't want her takin' walkies, Ethel.' He explained that the child would have to get used to being indoors during licensing hours. 'I thought if maybe you just sat with her, you know, keepin' her company, she wouldn't mind bein' kept in. It's only for today. You could still nip over to check on your old man.'

'Well, yes, fine . . .' Ethel picked up her glass and frowned. 'What'll she do after today?'

'Kids catch on fast. She's nearly five, so she's big enough to bowl about the place on her own – down here,

135

that is. In a couple of weeks the play group on Milton Street's startin' up again, so that'll solve the problem. Today, because it's special, I don't want her in the way an' kickin' up a fuss about goin' out.'

Ethel told him she'd be happy to oblige. The glass was halfway to her lips again when Angie reappeared, her eyes blazing.

'Den. Can I have a word?'

'Have as many as you like, petal.'

'Through here.'

Ethel stood enthralled as Den followed Angie through to the back and walked straight into her rage. There wasn't any need for Ethel to strain her ears. Angie seemed to think that because she couldn't be seen, she couldn't be heard.

'Do you think I was blowin' through a hole in me chest when I was talkin' about our private quarters?'

'It's only for today – '

'Over my dead body.'

'Let's not start about your dead body, Ange. I know enough about that already, don't I? I've slept next to it often enough.'

'You don't care about my privacy or anythin' else I want, do you?' she screeched. 'I don't want anybody up there! I told you as much!'

Den groaned. 'So what *do* you want? Eh? It's openin' day. You made no bloody arrangements about the kid. So I did. What's the alternative? Do you want her screamin' her head off all the time while we're tryin' to establish a good image with the punters? Is that the sort of start to make, I ask you?'

As the row progressed, Ethel noted, it kept wandering off the topic. When Den tried to stick to his point, Angie kept throwing up other things. His stupidity about paperwork came into it, his thoughtlessness when they were out together, even his sloppiness in the bathroom.

136

Angie clearly wanted to tell Den everything she disliked or hated about him; the disagreement about young Sharon, Ethel reckoned, was just an excuse for a discharge of abuse.

When it was Den's turn to go on the attack, as Ethel would later tell it to her friend Louise, the air turned blue. The bulk of his invective seemed to centre on Angie's sexuality. He criticized her appearance, telling her she looked like ten-bob tart. Her manner with strange men, he said, reminded him of a bitch on heat. As a wife and soul mate, on the other hand, she displayed all the charm and allure of a chewed grey vest.

It went on and on. The business about Sharon was abandoned completely as the acrimony mounted. Ethel had never heard anything like it. Finally, when Angie had told Den he was so gutter-muck thick he couldn't find his own arse with both hands, a silence fell. Ethel waited, her glass midway between the bar and her mouth. Angie appeared in the doorway, flushed, her eyes hard as bullets.

'Forget about lookin' after Sharon,' she said. 'We've come up with another arrangement.'

'It wouldn't be no trouble . . .'

'No, it's all right. We'll cope.' Angie snatched a bottle of Guinness off the shelf. 'Have another drink.'

A half hour passed before Den finally thought he should make a move towards conciliation, if only in the interests of business. Angie's brightness hadn't flagged as she served customer after customer, but her manner was so brittle it looked as if she might split at any second.

During a lull Den pulled her aside. 'Friends, eh?'

'Piss off.'

'Oh, come on, Ange. So we had a row. So what? It was all about nothin', as usual.'

He edged her through the doorway to the foot of the

137

stairs and pecked her cheek. Angie shook herself free and went back to the bar. Den stepped behind her.

'I'm sorry,' he murmured close to her ear. 'I apologize.'

'So you bloody should.'

'And so I bloody did.' He patted her backside. 'Look, if you want me to cancel Ethel's job, I'll do it. It's not important enough to get us battlin' like that.'

When Angie looked at him he could see she had softened. A little.

'It's not that I don't like the old girl,' she said huffily. 'It's just that I'd rather we had a stranger, somebody not from round here . . .'

Although he had no intention of getting anyone else, Den nodded sympathetically.

'Yeah, I see your point. The only reason I wanted Ethel, to tell you the truth . . .' He stopped and sighed, as if he were reluctant to go on.

Angie went along the bar to serve a customer, then came back and urged him to say his piece.

'Well, she's got a terrible life. There's only her money goin' into the home, if you can call it a home. She don't get no luxuries, no treats, no nothin' – just the day-in, day-out grind of hardship. All the company she's got is old William, an' he hasn't the puff even to speak to her, half the time. He's all she's got an' by the looks of him she won't have him much longer. Ethel leads a life of misery and boredom, Angie. I thought a job in the pub would be just the thing. Somethin' for her to look forward to each day. A break from the misery, know what I mean? A little drop of sunshine.'

Angie said nothing. She wiped up a couple of glasses, smiled and waved goodbye to some customers, pulled a pint of bitter for one of the men from the market.

'I'll let her do a shift tomorrow an' tell her that's it,' Den said, pretending to check the number of mixers on the cold shelf.

138

Angie turned to him. 'Look, all that stuff I said before – forget it.'

'What?' Den's face was all innocent confusion. 'But you said – '

'Never mind what I said.' She sighed. 'I tend to think about meself too much, as you never stop tellin' me. Well this time I'm not thinkin' about me. Let Ethel keep the job.'

'Are you sure, now?'

'I'm sure. It's right what you said, after all. She's got a rotten life. The least we can do is help to put a bit of variety into it.' She smiled. 'There's times, I suppose, when we need the likes of Ethel to remind us just how well-off we are.'

In the flat, Ethel had brought William his favourite lunch – scrambled egg and soldiers of toast. As she set it on his lap and plumped the cushions behind him, she glanced across at the pub and shook her head.

'What is it, love?' William's voice was very weak now, a trickling thread of sound that barely passed his lips.

'Them,' Ethel said. 'Young Den and Angie.'

William teased at the rubbery egg with his fork. 'What about them?'

'I never saw a couple like them. I don't know what holds them together.'

'Love,' William said.

'There's no love there,' Ethel sighed. 'Nor any respect. Maybe hate holds some people together – that pair seem to hate each other's guts somethin' rotten.' She reached out and touched William's cheek. 'I'm ever so pleased we're us,' she said.

He smiled at her. 'It's hardly ideal, Ethel. Me stuck in a chair all day, you out workin'. It's not the life I'd have picked . . .'

'If it had turned out only half as good, William, it'd still be a lot better than some people have got.' She gazed at him fondly. 'I'm glad it was you I married. Gladder than I can tell you.'

William put down his fork. He reached out and took her hand. 'I'm the one that's been lucky.'

She clasped both hands around his fingers. 'We're both lucky. We're happy, we've always been happy. We've been blessed with havin' each other all this time.' She looked across at the pub again. 'When I think of the rotten lives some folk have, it makes me want to get on my knees an' give thanks.'

# 14

Arthur Fowler's mind was set against any confrontation with the supernatural. 'You shouldn't tamper,' he told Pauline. 'It's meant to be left alone.' Arthur had once looked it up, and he'd taken the trouble to memorize the definition. 'Matters that can only be explained by the powers of spirits and superior beings,' he said. 'Experiences connected with forces unknown to man. Now what right have we to go diggin' into the likes of that? There's no sayin' what you could unleash.'

'You're makin' too much of it,' Pauline said.

'Am I? Listen, Hitler was into all that hocus-pocus an' mystic powers bit. You know what a bloody nutter he was – an' look where it got him.'

'We're not plannin' another world war,' Louise pointed out. 'We're just havin' a session with the tea leaves.'

Pauline nodded. 'Ethel's good at it, Arthur, you've got to hand her that. Remember when I was carryin' Mark, she told me we was goin' to have a boy?'

'An' she reckoned it'd be a boy second time, too,' Arthur reminded her. 'She's not all that good. The point is, she shouldn't be tinkerin' with the unknown, an' you shouldn't be aidin' an' abettin' her.'

'You go over to the pub an' leave us to it,' Louise told him sternly.

'Sounds like a fair enough idea to me,' Arthur said, taking his jacket off the back of the kitchen door. 'Just don't go sendin' Ethel across to read the froth in the bottom of me glass.'

When Arthur had gone Louise cleared the table in the front room and covered it with a fresh white cloth. On these occasions she liked to observe ritual. The drill was to have a clean, starched cloth, the best china cups and saucers, and a tray in the centre for the teapot, sugar and milk. The careful arrangement elevated the atmosphere, dispelling any air of triviality.

'There.' Louise set down the last cup and saucer and stood back.

'How much is this settin' you back, Mum?'

'Two quid. She didn't want to charge me, seein' as I'm her best friend, but I insisted. That's her usual fee, anyway, an' Ethel needs all the pennies she can lay her hands on.'

The session had been arranged the day before, when Louise had told Ethel that it was time she had some kind of notion how things would be going for the family over the next year or so. There was far too much uncertainty at present. Arthur was in danger of being made redundant; young Michelle, five now, was having one bout of illness after another; Pauline suffered terribly disturbed nights and Louise suspected her own rheumatics were getting worse.

'It doesn't hurt to know a bit of what's ahead,' she muttered, straightening a corner of the cloth. 'Whatever Arthur says, I still believe that forewarned is forearmed. An, if there's a bit of good luck to look forward to, it's all the better to know about it. Keeps you goin', doesn't it?'

In her flat at number 1B Ethel was setting everything out for William. On the table beside his chair he had the newspaper, his reading glasses, the little bottle with the tablets he had to take six times a day and the tiny transistor radio Ethel had got for him off a stall in the market.

'Now is there anythin' else you want?'

William shook his head. 'You've done me proud, Ethel.'

She leaned over him and tucked the blanket in at his

sides. 'I shouldn't be more than an hour. Less, if it all goes smoothly.'

William turned his weary eyes towards her and smiled. 'Are you in good form?'

'How d'you mean?'

'Are the spirits strong?' He always made gentle fun of Ethel's psychic talents.

'Strong as they need to be.' She kissed his cheek. 'Remember the football's on later – I've set the wireless on the right station for you.'

She got her coat and hat. 'Don't go doin' no acrobatics while I'm out,' she said, chuckling. 'When I get back I'll start on our tea. Meat an' potato pie. That'll put some colour in your cheeks.' She perched her hat on her head and put on her coat, then kissed William again and went out.

On the way across to Louise's house she wondered if she should have a little drink first. It sometimes helped to lubricate her visions. She paused and looked at the pub, as if it were daring her to walk past.

'Just one,' she muttered and hurried across to the door.

'Oh God, she's come after me,' Arthur moaned as she came in. 'The witch of Walford.' He was leaning against the bar with his brother-in-law, Pete Beale. 'I'm goin' to have to buy some garlic off your stall, Pete. Make meself a necklace with it.'

'You're always takin' the mickey, Arthur,' Ethel said as she stepped up to the bar, brandishing a folded pound note. 'One of these days you might be glad of my talent. I could save you from makin' a blunder or two.'

'Tell you what, Ethel,' Arthur said. 'I'll buy you a Guinness if you'll promise not to put a curse on me.'

'Leave it out, Arthur,' Pete said softly. 'She gets the piss taken out of her enough as it is.'

Nowadays, Pete was a firm believer in Ethel's ability with palm-reading and tea leaves. She had recently told him he was going to have an ugly, unavoidable experience. The next day he bumped into his first wife and her mother outside a supermarket. He had been the recipient of some impromptu and highly embarrassing sarcasm.

'I'm only havin' a bit of fun,' Arthur said. He turned to Ethel. 'I'll get the drink, love. The usual?'

'Ta.' She went to the corner of the bar and propped herself. 'Has Louise an' your Pauline got everythin' ready?'

'The temple's been set up, yeah. They'd a bit of trouble findin' a goat to slaughter, but the butcher helped them out.'

'It's a serious occasion,' Ethel said firmly.

'If you say so.' Arthur ordered a Guinness from Den. When it was served up he handed it across to Ethel. 'There you go.' He watched her take her first thirsty gulp. 'Did they say just why they want you to have a gander into the future, Ethel? I mean, is there somethin' I've not been told?'

'They just want to know what direction things'll be takin' – well, Lou does, anyway.'

'What about yourself, Ethel?' Pete asked her.

'What about me?'

'Do you ever check up on your own future?'

'Yes, I do. Regularly.'

'Everythin' all right, is it?'

She stared at her drink. 'As good as can be expected at my age, an' William's.'

The truth was otherwise. For months, Ethel had been able to raise no insight about herself or William. She had tried, many times, but nothing happened. She failed, at every attempt, to gain even a glint of what lay in store. The special feeling never came, that sense of treading forward in time and being granted a vision of what lay before her.

'I wish to God I could do that,' Pete said. 'It'd be great

144

to know what I could afford an' what I couldn't. As it is I keep makin' predictions, spendin' money I haven't got an' windin' up never gettin' it.'

Ethel hadn't heard him. Two strange things had happened. The last mouthful of her drink tasted metallic; she had nearly gagged on it. Secondly, she had an overwhelming, dizzying feeling that some powerful insight was on its way. She felt a little worried for Louise. The foretaste was a dark one. She put the half-full glass back on the counter.

'Sorry about leavin' some, Arthur. I just wasn't in the mood for it, after all.'

Both men watched as she waved absently to Den and left.

Pete blinked at Arthur. 'That was a bit sudden, wasn't it?'

'Never saw her leave a drink before,' Arthur said. 'Maybe she left her broomstick on double yellows.' He reached for Ethel's glass and set it down alongside his own. 'Waste not, want not, as they say.'

Ethel hurried across to number 45 and let herself in by the kitchen door. Louise was by the cooker putting the lid on a pan of peeled potatoes, ready for boiling later.

'Is the kettle on?' Ethel asked her, banging the door shut.

'I was waitin' till you got here.' She frowned. 'What's up, Et? You look a bit flustered.'

'Nothin's up.' Ethel's face contradicted her. 'I'll take me coat off, while you're gettin' ready.' Pauline came into the kitchen and was nearly knocked over by the little woman as she strode through the door, slipping off her coat as she went.

'What's up with her?'

Louise shrugged. 'Got a mood on, by the looks of it.' She picked up the kettle. 'I'll put out some digestive

145

biscuits. That'll put her in a better frame of mind. Loves a digestive, does Ethel.'

As they sat down round the table a few minutes later, Ethel maintained an introspective silence. She didn't speak unless she was spoken to, and her retorts were brief and vague. She finished her tea quickly and sat back, her hands restless on the tablecloth.

'Et, are you sure you're all right?' Louise asked her.

'Fine. I'm just anxious to get started.'

This wasn't the usual procedure. Normally they would sit round the table taking their time over the tea, chatting about their aspirations and plans for the future. That was how the scene was set. The atmosphere of looking forward led nicely into Ethel's readings. Today she didn't seem to want to communicate. She was pale and edgy, casting wary glances at Louise every few seconds. She hadn't even taken a biscuit.

When the cups were drained Ethel grabbed Louise's first. She inverted it and turned it three times on the saucer, fearful of what she would see. When she looked, all she saw was a splash of tea leaves. Puzzled, she let her eyes go out of focus. What she saw then was an out-of-focus splash of tea leaves. She frowned and shook her head.

'What is it?' Pauline asked huskily.

Ethel didn't reply. She turned the cup between her hands. It could be a bush, perhaps. Or a tree. It could be anything. This was all wrong, she thought. The image was usually followed by a sharp interpretation. It was automatic.

Louise leaned forward. 'What do you see, Et?'

For a moment it resembled a bear's head, but not very convincingly. Ethel narrowed her eyes, concentrating hard. It was a tree again, then it wasn't. In truth, the deposit in the cup resembled nothing more than a clotted mess of tea leaves.

146

'I'm havin' some trouble,' she said. Her head was beginning to hurt. So were her eyes. There was no way, it seemed, to visualize anything but a brown clot. She had never known herself to be so stumped for an insight. 'I think I'll leave yours for a minute, Lou.'

She started on Pauline's cup. How could this be, she wondered. She had known, beyond a shadow of doubt, that she would have a rivetingly clear vision at this session. Instead, she was beginning to feel that her powers had deserted her.

'Well now, Pauline . . .'

This looked like a star, she thought, with some stardust trailing behind it, reaching to the lip of the cup. But no interpretation offered itself. From another angle it looked like a splodgy apple. *This is stupid*! Ethel thought angrily. She turned the cup and turned it again. The remains didn't look like anything now. There was no image, no foresight.

She banged the cup down on the table.

'Et . . .'

'I'm sorry.' She felt tears welling. She rubbed her eyes and snatched up the cup again. Her vision swam, then there was a terrible pain behind her eyes. She felt the blood drain from her face and hands.

Pauline stood up. 'I'll get a glass of water . . .'

Ethel looked terrible. She had gone white and her lips were trembling.

'My God.' Louise reached across and touched her friend's arm. 'What's got into you, girl?'

'I'm . . .'

She had meant to say, again, that she was all right. But the power of speech left her. As her head began to spin she looked up at the wall above the fireplace and felt the sudden onrush, the surge of revelation. She saw a black circle, fuzzy-edged. A hole. A moment later a voice, William's voice, spoke her name.

Ethel shot to her feet and hurled herself towards the kitchen. She collided with the door jamb. Off-balance, moaning, she made it to the rear door and pulled it open.

'Ethel . . .'

Pauline tried to get hold of her but she was gone, slamming the yard door against the wall as she ran out on to Bridge Street. At the corner she stopped. Pete Beale came out of the pub and saw her. He stepped close.

'What's wrong, Ethel? You look bad, love.'

He folded his arm around her shoulder. Ethel was staring across at her living room window. Her mouth was working, making tiny, catlike sounds.

'Let's sit you on a crate for a minute, eh?'

She let out a sudden, terrible howl and broke away from Pete. Stumbling, tripping, she made her way across to the steps outside the flat and gripped the railing.

'William!'

She ran up the steps. The door had been left on the latch. She rushed inside and threw open the door to the living room. William was still in his chair, gazing down at the newspaper spread open on his knees. His reading glasses were perched on the end of his nose.

Ethel went to the chair and knelt beside him. His eyes moved. She touched his hand and felt the terrible coldness.

'Oh, William . . .'

His eyes began to close, then jerked open again. He drew back his head sharply, making his glasses fall off. He looked at her.

'My darlin',' Ethel whispered. 'Darlin' . . .'

She reached out and held him by the shoulders. He took a long, slow breath. His tongue protruded from his lips. He seemed about to speak, but then his teeth clamped together and his mouth widened in a grimace of pain.

Ethel grabbed the bottle of tablets and fought with the

cap. She unscrewed it and let it fall. Tipping a dozen tablets on to her hand she snatched one and pushed it at William's lips. The muscles were so rigid she couldn't get past them.

'Take it, please take it!'

She shoved so hard the tablet crumbled. She took another one and the same thing happened. William was staring at her now, beseeching her. A shudder of panic passed through Ethel and she dropped the tablets.

'Dear Jesus . . .'

Louise walked into the room and saw Ethel on all fours, trying to pick up the scattered tablets. She strode forward quickly and caught the little woman by the arms.

'Steady, love. Steady.'

On her knees, Ethel looked up at William. The pain had gone from his face. His eyes were still open, but they were sightless. She put out her hand and touched his cool cheek.

'Oh, my poor William . . .'

Louise held her tightly as she began to cry, the grief choking her, scrambling her voice.

'There, Ethel. There now.'

Louise patted her, trying to soothe her the way she did with her grandchildren. As she drew Ethel's head towards her breast one word escaped through the sobbing. It sounded like 'infinity', but Louise couldn't be sure.

# 15

'He that dwelleth in the secret place of the most High shall abide under the shadow of the Almighty,' the minister intoned. 'I will say of the Lord, He is my refuge and my fortress, my God: In him will I trust.'

It was raining. The mourners around the grave were huddled under umbrellas, their collars turned up against the swirling wind. Some were looking towards the minister, others gazed at the ground; most of them stared towards the varnished coffin, hearing the rain drum on the lid. Ethel stood nearest the grave, clad entirely in black. A net veil obscured her face. Throughout the service she had been staring at the brass plate on the coffin, watching the engraved words and figures trap the raindrops.

WILLIAM EDWARD
SKINNER
1915–1975

It seemed such a tiny compass of years. William's entire life had occupied an insignificant space of time, yet it had left a crop of memories that seemed endless as they teemed through Ethel's mind. Today she could only remember him being young, the handsome, smiling man in his twenties who had approached her one day by a dreary little municipal pond. The man who had changed her life, the dear soul whose love, for all the ensuing years, had made her feel safe.

Ethel didn't feel safe any more. She was alone again. She had forgotten what a cold feeling that was. The fear had come and gone in her all day, the anticipation of William being consigned to that cold grave, gone from her forever.

'What am I goin' to do?' she had asked Louise.

'You're strong, Ethel. You'll bear up.'

'I've nobody to be strong *for*, any more.'

The thought lingered. There lay William, about to be interred. Here stood his Ethel, lost, bereft of a vital part of herself. What purpose did she have any more? There was no one to cherish, no person cherishing her. She remembered the frightful early days in Hackney during the war, the bereaved time when she moved from one threshold of panic to the next. She was back in that state, a woman without purpose and empty of hope.

Louise, standing behind Ethel, reached forward and touched her arm. 'You all right, love?' she whispered.

Ethel nodded.

'Unto thee will I cry, Oh Lord my rock,' the minister said. 'Be not silent to me, lest if thou be silent to me I become like them that go down into the pit.'

Pit was just the word, Ethel thought. William would be put in one pit, she would live in another, a chasm of longing, an abyss of isolation. She had never known anything like this. She wasn't just the way she had been in those dark times in Hackney. Then she had suffered a terrible loss, it was true, but now she had lost the precious jewel of her life. Her lovely William was dead, and now she entertained the thought, as she had many times over the last four days, that she should waste no time in joining him.

She had even considered the ways. There was an old bottle of lysol in the flat. There were still William's pills, bottles of them. There were knives, a couple of razors – to find a method of going was no problem. What held her back, as it had yesterday and early this morning, was the thought of William's disapproval.

'I never understood anybody takin' their own lives,' he had once said to her. 'However bad anythin' is, there's always life, isn't there? You can't go back on suicide. It's too final. I reckon anybody that takes their life has forgotten what curiosity is. I mean, whatever happened, I'd still like to be around for the upshot. It's a crime to throw life away. A crime, Ethel.'

But she wanted to throw it away, discard it, have done with the pain. What was left to her? A life alone in the flat, passing days without any purpose, pining for times that were dead and gone. As the ropes around the coffin tautened and the box was lifted clear of its supports, Ethel believed she was prepared to put up with William's severest chiding. She wanted to be with him, whatever the price. Nothing could be worse than the emptiness and the encroaching fear.

The coffin was lowered into the grave. Ethel watched it disappear and felt the final tearing loss. As she swayed backwards, abandoning herself to the shrouding despair, Louise caught her by the arm and drew her close.

'Hang on, love. Hang on.'

The rest of the day was a haze of events that came nowhere near to touching Ethel. She sat in a corner of her flat, staring at William's empty chair as people sipped sherry, whispered to each other and cast worried glances in her direction. Dr Legg, who had made all the funeral arrangements, sat beside her for a time and explained that he would like her to stay on in the flat. He didn't want rent; if Ethel would continue to do the cleaning and act as caretaker, they would be quits. The place was hers for as long as she would ever want it.

None of that penetrated. Ethel was aware that she was making the proper responses, but it was something she didn't control. Her shell, the outward Ethel, was operating by itself. Her spirit, or whatever that hurting thing was at her centre, stood on a cold promontory of

152

grief and longed for things to be as they had been. Without William, life had no value or purpose. No kindness or concern could reach her.

Louise had decided she would stay with her friend for a few nights. On the third evening, as she brought them cocoa from the kitchen, she watched Ethel sidelong. It was like sharing a room with a mute. Pale and motionless, Ethel gave the impression that she had entered a trance state. As Louise approached, she decided firmly that it was her duty to do something drastic, before despondency isolated her friend for good.

'Get that down you, Ettie.'

Ethel had been staring at the transistor radio on the table in the corner. It was still set to the station for the Saturday football commentary. William had never found out how West Ham did that day. She glanced at Louise, irritated slightly by her briskness.

'I don't want any, ta.'

The cup was placed firmly, almost forcibly into her hand. 'Drink it,' Louise snapped.

'I told you – '

'You listen to me, Ethel May Skinner.' Louise dropped into the chair opposite and glared at her. 'I've had nothin' but silence and mopin' out of you since I came here. You're soaked in self-pity. I'm not havin' it. What you need is something hot in you an' a damned good talkin' to.'

Ethel stared at the cup. The smell of chocolate made her feel sick. 'Lou, I can't drink this . . .'

'Make yourself. You haven't eaten a bite nor touched more than the odd cup of tea for nearly a week.'

'My stomach's not right . . .'

'It's your head what ain't right. Now listen to me. I've been watchin' you carefully, for days now. You're driftin' away from us. You're slidin' outside of all that's goin' on. It's got to stop.'

153

'Just leave me, Lou.' It was meant to be an irritable retort. It came out as no more than a petulant whine.

Louise sipped from her cup and sat back in the chair. 'Do you remember when my Albert passed away?'

Ethel looked at her, feeling as if she were beyond a sheet of thick glass. 'Lou, I don't want to talk, or listen . . .'

'I didn't know what to do with meself,' Louise went on, as if she hadn't heard. 'It was like I'd lost a leg. I couldn't cope. The kids did what they could, bless them, but I was that heartbroken nothin' seemed to console me. Then you took me on one side. Remember?'

Ethel found herself responding to memory. She saw the front room at number 45, the kids on the couch, Louise sitting by the fireplace putting a balled handkerchief to her eyes.

'I remember it, Lou.'

'What did you say to me?'

Ethel tried to recall her words. They hadn't been planned, she had just reacted impatiently to Louise's gloom and misery. 'I can't remember . . .'

'You told me I was like a wet weekend. You told me to buck meself up an' start behavin' like the person I was. On top of that you said Albert would be ashamed of me.'

Ethel was staring at the mantelpiece now. There was a picture of herself and William, taken on the night of their silver wedding party.

'Are you listenin', Et?'

'Yes.'

'So what would William be thinkin', if he could see you now?'

'Maybe he can see me, Lou.' Ethel turned sad, dark-rimmed eyes to her friend. 'I do have the feelin' he's there, somewhere.'

154

'All right.' Louise put down her cup and folded her arms. 'So what *is* he thinkin'?'

'I don't know. It isn't clear, it's just a feelin' . . .' She closed her eyes tightly. 'Lou, I want to be with William. I don't want to be on me own without him.'

'You've got to take the world the way it comes,' Louise said. 'If we live our lives right we'll get our hearts' desire, I've always believed that. I don't know nothin' about heaven an' the hereafter, but I do know there's a right way to do things, to make life turn out for the best.'

For the first time since William died, Ethel felt a spark of curiosity. Was life built like that, she wondered. Did you have to pass all these tests first, then get your reward? Albert had gone to his reward, so had William. Here were their wives; given any chance at all, they would be with the men they loved. But there was no easy way – at least that was the notion Louise had planted.

'Maybe . . .'

Louise leaned forward, encouraged by the concentration on Ethel's face. 'Maybe what, love?'

'They're just waitin' for us. That could be it. It's not a matter of them goin' far away. They step outside the room we call life, an' they wait. We've got to finish the job we were put here to do, before we join up with them. We mustn't break the rules.'

'It's a nice thought,' Louise said.

A dark fantasy played itself swiftly across Ethel's mind. She pictured herself taking her own life, then being condemned to another place, billions of miles from the patiently-waiting William, because she had cheated.

'Here's somethin' else to think about,' Louise said softly. 'If you're sure he's near you, where's the heartbreak?'

'Do you think he really is near, Lou? Or am I just bein' fanciful?'

'He's not lost, Ettie. You've got the power to know

155

things like that. If you feel your William's near you, then he is. An' from now on there's nothin' bad can happen to him. He's run all his risks an' had all his hard times. Now he's there waitin' for you. When you've paid your dues you'll be with him.'

Infinity, Ethel thought. Endless space and time. Now, blindingly, she saw what it meant, the startling omen she'd had all those years before. There was a time when you were apart from the one you loved, but it was only a moment, then you were rejoined for ever and ever. She could believe that.

'Lou.'

'What, love?'

'I want to stay here on me own tonight.'

Louise frowned at her. 'Why? What've you got in mind?'

'I want to talk to William, an' I think I can do it better if there's just the two of us in the place, me an' him.'

Louise stared at her. Ethel looked very sincere. There was nothing evasive in her eyes. 'Promise me you're not goin' to do anythin' silly?'

'I wouldn't dare, now.'

Pauline was in the kitchen as Louise came in through the back door. 'Not stoppin' with Ethel tonight, then?'

Louise put down the carrier bag with her night things in it. 'No need any more,' she said.

'Is she comin' out of it?'

'She'll be right as rain.' The cocoa had left a cloying taste in Louise's mouth. 'Goin' to make us a brew, eh? I just fancy a nice cup of tea, then a good night's sleep in me own bed.'

Pauline picked up the kettle and started filling it. 'You said she'd snap out of her gloom eventually, didn't you?'

Louise nodded. 'For a time there, though, I thought she wasn't goin' to make it. I could see her headin' the way a lot of them do.'

'What brought her round, then?'

'Somethin' I said. Somethin' she thought up for herself. A bit of both.' She smiled. 'To tell you the truth, it might have been a lot of baloney, for all I know. But she's on the mend. I could see it on her face.'

'That's good.'

Louise eased off her coat. 'It's what me gran always used to say. Any medicine's good, if it works.' She smiled again. 'I'd be a real happy woman if I could believe half the codswallop Ethel's got into her head. But it's worked. I'm sure it has.'

On the following Monday Angie Watts hauled herself out of bed at half-past eight, blinking and grumbling. She had been snatched from a dream of opulence and wellbeing by a terrible racket at the bottom of the stairs.

'What the hell's goin' on?' Belting her dressing gown, Angie went to the stairwell and scowled over the bannister. She saw the Hoover's power cable snaking through from the bar. 'Den? You down there?'

The sound was mechanical with a roughly musical background. As Angie made her way down, she realized that the vacuum cleaner's noise was being augmented by two human voices. In the passage at the foot of the stairs Ethel was hoovering vigorously and singing; Den was harmonizing from the bar.

'God almighty.'

Angie strode into the bar and landed an irritable punch on Den's arm. He turned, startled for a moment, then smiled at her.

'Mornin', Princess. I see the beauty sleep didn't work again.'

'What's the meanin' of all this flamin' row?'

'It's the sounds of industry, love. While you've been kippin' up there we've been scourin' the place.'

'Can't you do it a bit more quietly?'

157

'Ethel set the tone,' Den said, grinning. 'Loud an' lusty. It gets infectious after a bit.'

Angie went through to the back again. She tapped Ethel on the shoulder and pointed to the Hoover. Ethel smiled amiably and switched it off.

'Mornin', Angie.'

'Mornin', Ethel. Do you think you could keep that thing quiet until I've got a cup of coffee inside me? It's playin' hell with me nerves.'

Ethel considered the request, then nodded. 'Fair enough. I can get on with the polishin'.' She pushed the Hoover against the wall and took her little work box from the table by the telephone. She hesitated, then put the box down again. 'Tell you what. I'll give the door mats a bit of a bang, first.' She flashed her dentures at the rumpled Angie. 'Do things in a proper order, eh? It makes sense in the long run.'

'Whatever you say, Ethel,' Angie groaned, heading back upstairs.

A few minutes later Dr Legg saw Ethel as he drove along Bridge Street. She was energetically slamming a doormat against the wall of the pub, surrounding herself with a cloud of yellowy dust. Harold stopped the car and got out.

'Ethel,' he said brightly, avoiding the cloud. 'How are you?'

She let the mat drop and reached for another one from the pile beside her. 'Fit as a horse thank you, Doctor.'

The last time he spoke to her she had been despondent and not in a mood to talk. 'This is quite a change, I must say.'

Ethel stepped closer. 'I'm sorry if I was a bit difficult, before.' She fingered a speck of dust from her eye. 'I wasn't thinkin' straight.'

'Perfectly understandable. I'll admit I thought it'd be a

while before you started picking up. Bereavement's never easy for anyone.'

'Oh, I don't think I'll stop missin' William. But I've got me plans laid. Got meself a sense of direction. I'll cope, Doctor.'

Harold smiled. 'And what plans have you cooked up?'

'Oh, simple enough. See, for a while there I couldn't see any point in goin' on. But Lou sorted me out. There definitely is a point in goin' on. I'm on my way somewhere, after all. An' there's a great day at the end of me journey.'

Harold wondered briefly if she had been in touch with an evangelist. 'I must say you're looking well.'

'Feelin' grand, Doctor. Back on me old form.'

'Did you give any more thought to my suggestion about taking a few days away somewhere?'

She nodded. 'I thought about it, but there's no need for a break. I've lots to do right here, an' that's holiday enough for me.' She waved an arm towards the square. 'I help old Mrs Turner out Tuesdays an' Thursdays, Mr Craig needs help with his leg bandages every mornin', I give Lou a hand with the washin' three or four times a week, an then there's me paid jobs. I've no time to get mopey. No reason, either.'

'Well, there's nothing like doing whatever makes you feel good, Ethel.'

She nodded firmly. 'I told meself this – I have to keep on. It's all a journey, like I just said. So that's what I'll do, I'll keep on keepin' on.' She chuckled and took a grip on the end of the door mat. 'Everybody's auntie, that's me.'

Harold moved away. 'I'll see you later, Ethel. Pop in and have coffee after surgery.'

'If I've time, Doctor.' She waggled her head at him cheerily and began banging the mat on the wall, setting up another dust cloud.

Harold got back in the car and started the engine. He watched Ethel for a moment, marvelling at the energy in the tiny figure. Everybody's auntie, he thought warmly. The description fitted her to a tee. He recalled how worried William had been, wondering if Ethel would manage on her own. He could certainly rest in peace on that score.

'Good old Ethel,' Harold murmured, engaging the gears. It was soothing to think that some things in Albert Square just wouldn't change, no matter what.